Thanks

To everyone who encouraged me, especially my mom.

BROKEN HUMANITY

By *Faissal Alchaar*

FSC
www.fsc.org
MIX
Papper från ansvarsfulla källor
Paper from responsible sources
FSC® C105338

Förlag: BoD – Books on Demand, Stockholm, Sverige
Tryck: BoD – Books on Demand, Norderstedt, Tyskland

ISBN: 9789180076678

I. Nopoly

1- Just a Regular Day

I'm chilling on my couch while holding a little baby to my chest.

"Where is your careless mommy?" I say to this baby who is eating my finger; it's so sweet. I raise my head at the window in the room, and I realize that the sun is shining; it's the sunrise. The glow starts growing stronger, and when the sky turns to a warm white light, I come closer to the open window to close it, but a blinding flash stops me. I try to protect my eyes with my hand from the harmful light; that light wakes me up to see that the sunshine that is hitting my face is the reason for that terrible dream.

It is Friday morning, and I gotta get up to welcome my new day with a smile while I'm seeing the sunlight come through my window. The view is so fabulous from my apartment, so I am used to going out to my balcony every morning to catch some fresh air before starting my day. It'll be another nice day today; I can feel it in my bones.

Seeing the people walk with their nineteenth century fashion suits, with that classic music that is playing everywhere, makes me move like I'm dancing while I'm preparing myself to go out to my beautiful city, Nopoly.

I always start my day with a cup of tea before I go to work; the tea that comes from Idan country. Idan is so far away from here and full of demons, unfortunately, which makes things harder and full of danger for our Explorers Army. I have to stop thinking about that now and focus on the newspaper I am holding for a while.

The newspapers are always full of good news, which makes me feel safe to live here. Having the best industry and highly advanced health care are the main topics; and there is either a nice article or a short poem at the end of the newspaper, which is what really makes me read it.

Today's poem is named "Well":

"*Well, everything is well*

Very good buy for what you sell

Call us in a hurry if you feel so ill

Sing the song and repeat the tell

Pray for science, and break the bell

Remember that you always have the will

So, you are fine and free but still, so well."

I don't think my crazy dreams or the voice in my head are sicknesses, right? So, I don't need to call anyone at this moment, but now it feels like I'm crazy to talk to myself.

"No, you are not, but . . ." I shake my head to avoid the voice and start to look at the incredible view that I see from my balcony. Such an advantage to live on the sixth floor in a wondrous city like this.

I'm taking out my clothes like a knight taking out his sword; it's known that a man needs to practice his job before starting it. After a conversation with myself, I head to the bathroom to take a lovely warm shower before putting my clothes on.

My entertainment of modifying the "Well" poem to become a funny song with some editing from me, even though my voice isn't particularly good, has stopped when I finish my shower. Good thing that my choice of clothes is better than my voice quality. I know that even without a mirror; there is no mirror in the entire city, but that's okay because I dress just like the others; nineteenth century fashion.

I jump on my vehicle, which is drawn by a noble horse named Areo, to go to my workplace.

"I don't think he likes to draw your heavy wagon."

"It's its job to . . . Eh, I'm getting sick of you," I whisper, putting my hand on my forehead at the silliness of this conversation on this lovely morning.

"And it's your job to be conned." My talker brain starts arguing. This voice makes me feel I'm crazy, especially because it sounds soft and creepy.

"Conned? I really want to smash you."

"Do it!"

"The thing is I don't want to break my beautiful Roman nose; so, no . . ."

The freshness everywhere with all these colors on buildings and the positive energy in the atmosphere make me feel good vibes I want to share with my lovely neighbor, who is passing by with so much joy on his face.

"But wait, doesn't that sound silly?" That voice comes into my head again.

"Do not start bothering me now. Let me have some peace and quiet today without your babbling!" I whisper to myself while covering my mouth with my coat.

"Okay."

I try to consider the beauty in this city and salute the walkers, the sellers, and the other riders on the street to ignore my talking brain. The impact of my talker is following me even when I sleep.

Every day I see dreams and I can't remember all of them, but the effect of them is still circling inside my head somehow. I remember one of them was about the war that started in my country; I saw dead bodies everywhere, and a large number of crying kids were creepily standing around me. That night, I woke up terrified by the nightmare with a racing heartbeat and sweaty body.

The police station is getting closer, and as soon as I arrive, the officer says to me:

"Good morning Mr. Cooper."

"Good morning."

I get in the building, and Marsen is standing outside my office, as always.

"Good morning captain. All papers are on the table."

"Thanks, go back to your work," I reply.

All the papers are full of information about how the police catch the sneaky demons who are trying to harm the people here; "our people." I raise my voice as an effective way to convince myself.

"Our?!"

"Yes. I live in this world, which means I live here with the rest in this city, so what's your problem?" I freak out at myself.

I do love this job, but it's quite boring to just sit in the office and sign for papers rather than explore this new world.

sty"One day, I'll be one of the Explorers Army to discover what could be outside the city and probably cut off some nasty demons' heads."

"Why all of this hate?"

"Because they are the enemy here," I answer my stupid head thinking about the demons, but I really feel safe living inside the city because everything is fine as long as we follow the law.

Every time I look at the horizon of Nopoly, I see the Plonsters at the top of the wall on the city's border. When I read about the Plonsters and how they appeared in this advanced city, I felt so grateful. They are the golden-winged guardians who are the sacrificed forms of all the gods in this universe. These gods decided to be inside seven Plonsters standing around Nopoly, and they have one job: to protect the city if the police and the army can't stop an attack from outside.

"This is the place of goodness and peace that I was looking for a long time . . ."

"It seems that you are happy here, more than in your previous life," my brain replies.

"It fits my thoughts and my personality, so yeah."

While I was trying to stop the conversation, a knock at the door did the trick.

"Come in," I reply.

"Excuse me, sir, General Charles D. Paul wants to talk to you," Marsen says.

"Yeah sure, let him in."

"Hello Captain Cooper, how are you my old friend?" the general says with a cigar in his mouth.

"Haha, old friend?! I'm good. What about you, general?"

"Good," he responds in his gruff voice, and continues, "I need backup for our army whose numbers were reduced after taking a bunch of my men to the Explorers test."

"Recruits for ExA are needed, right?" I ask hastily.

"Well, yes . . . They discovered a place full of energy that we need for our city, and they have a lack of explorers' numbers until now; that's what I heard. I came to you because you already have a good number in your service now; plus, it will be easier for a police officer to become a soldier rather than a civilian."

"And how many do you need, general?"

"Two hundred persons are all I need; is it okay for you?" He asks as if he already knows my answer.

"Sure, they are yours."

Now he is leaving with a smile on his face, a smile for our city and our future. After his departure, I consider the need for more members of the ExA; it could be my opportunity to be one of them, so I decide to write a letter to the commander of the Explorer Army telling him that I'm interested in joining the ExA.

After finishing the letter, I turn to see the lively city through the window, and then I switch my sights to the calendar while I grab a cigarette from my pocket; it's the sixth of August 2080.

A tapping on the door interrupts my conversation with my head that I'm having about the fashion the people have in this universe in 2080.

"Come in!" I shout.

"Sir, a guy has been caught trying to get out of the city," Marsen says.

"Bring him here and leave, please." The officer nods and closes the door.

Two minutes later Marsen returns with the guy. I look at the skinny man, raising my eyebrows, and ask him:

"What's your name?"

"Cason Baker," he answers immediately while I put the cigarette on the ashtray.

"Cason, why would you go out?"

"And why wouldn't I?" he answers politely.

"Don't you know what happens when someone goes out?"

"I know, but it's my life, my freedom, and I'll take the responsibility for my own choices. It won't affect anyone if I take the risk to go out!"

This man is starting to bother me, but I have to calm down and play the role of the captain.

"Don't you understand that there are millions of demons outside this damn city?" I continue.

"I know . . ."

"Haven't you seen them?"

"I have, but my . . ." and he stops talking.

"Look, my family, my friends, and my only love are outside, but I decided to leave them and live here; I would never go out to search for them because death is waiting for me if I think for a moment that I'm brave enough to show my face to these creatures." I say this, and I know deep inside me how much of a liar I am, thanks to my brain.

"But why do we have these things in this world?"

"This is their role in this life: to be murderers and kill us because we refuse to become just like them, so they're always waiting to take off . . ." and I pick up a horrible photo of a demon trying to take off someone's face. This is a picture I found in one of the books that I read from time to time. But the guy doesn't even react when he sees it! Even I can't stare at this photo like he does!

"What are you made of? Are you even a human? I know how I can fix you," I reply, and I open my mouth to shout to Marsen.

"That picture is from a book called *Innocent Sins*, and that's my brother who is in the picture, and . . . and to be honest I wanted to go out to find him because I miss him so much," the man says with a broken, sad voice.

"I understand your feelings, I'm sorry to hear that, but I think that he is ninety percent dead."

"We have the science, the power, and all the advantage to face these demons. Why do we have to just sit here without doing a thing, or to, at least, understand the reasons that make them do that?"

"We are doing our best," I interrupt him, then I call Marsen.

"Yes sir."

"Take him to Doctor Diana and let her help this guy."

"I don't need a doctor; I just need a hug maybe."

I stand up and come slowly to him with cold eyes, and I give him a hug.

"Go now with Marsen. I hope you will be fine, Mr. Baker."

"Thanks, sir."

I can see the confusion in Marsen because of what I've done, which is uncommon here, I think.

They are both leaving now, and I feel so itchy in my head.

"You knew that you lied."

"I had to," I try to convince myself.

*

The person who I exchanged lives with was a captain in the police, and the police's job here is to protect the people from any danger and stop them from doing things that may lead to forbidden acts. That's why they bring to my office the unusual people who come up with forbidden ideas, like getting out of the city or trying to fly in the city, which are forbidden for civilians for security reasons.

"You are doing a pretty good job, I suppose."

"When a man like me wants to live his life and never give in to death, that man will do whatever it takes to live with the new situation," I respond to my talker.

I finish my workday and head to my horse, which is waiting for me.

"Hungry huh? I'm starving buddy, let's get home fast so I can feed you, Areo." And I hit it with the whip.

"Feed him? Say that you want to eat and you need him to take you home, otherwise you'll be hungry. And that whip is hurting him . . . you know."

"I'm hungry, and guess what, I'm super selfish. It's just a horse, come on!" I scream in the middle of the street.

"Yeah, and you are just a doll."

"Can you stop, you troll? Because if you won't I'll go to Doctor Diana to fix you."

"Yeah, the doll needs to be fixed."

Riding among the colorful buildings that are like a rainbow and ignoring my talker makes me feel so good. I see the boys playing hopscotch on the sidewalk and laughing wholeheartedly.

"Don't you think you have to have a child though?"

"Who needs a child when the man has everything in this life, money, food, drinks, and sex?" I ask myself.

"Who said that?"

"This how it works for me here, so can you stop talking?"

On Sunday I'll go to the Temple of Science because all the people here do so. They go there to clean their brains, and that makes them impermeable from being affected by the demons' black magic. That's written in the *White Night Book*, which I read the first day I came here. The book gave me more knowledge of the way of life here and how the humans had lost most of the surface area of this Earth because of the demons, but Guider Dinis had saved humanity by building this city with the sacrifice of all the gods.

Nopoly exists to contain only the pure brains of people who believe only in science and nothing else. The amazing thing is that everyone loves each other here, and the only thing we hate in this world is demons because they are the first threat to the humans here, and everything that happens outside of Nopoly is because of the religious people who released these nasty monsters to kill those who don't agree with them. But they will never get us because we have the Bezman ideology, and that's why we practice our methodology in the Temple, which is a perfect place to make the brain feel better and stronger. All of this is recorded in the *White Night Book*, so I completely agree with it.

"What if—"

"No. You know, you are the second thing I hate after the damn demons." I shut my brain down.

What makes the Nopolyens see the demons is that they consider themselves followers of Bezman, which sanctifies the science that the demons hate and cannot stand up to. When one of those nasty demons is caught, by the police or soldiers, the demon become part of the circus after the chains are put around its neck, or the government takes it to be dissected to know more about these creatures and find a way to eliminate them forever.

Now I'm home, and I take Areo to the stable to eat some hay and drink water.

"That's my little big dude," I say, touching him.

I do care for Areo by myself because everyone is responsible for what he or she has here.

I finish my delicious meal, but my brain can’t stop talking; it’s going to be a long night.

2- A Secret for a Secret

Saturday is my favorite free day from work, but my brain doesn't understand that and keeps working still, so I try to keep it busy while I prepare breakfast.

Now I'm taking a cup of tea out to my beautiful balcony that is full of colorful flowers.

"What a lovely smell on the morning . . ."

"You have to love the smell of thinking critically as well!"

"I do. Why would you still be babbling now if I didn't?" I guess that I made it obvious to my brain now.

"There is a big difference between the brain that does the habit and the one that is thinking and arguing, right?'

"It feels so crazy to talk to myself!"

"No, it's not, Harley."

I open my eyes wide while the hot tea is spilling on the floor. I'm so shocked by what my brain called me, because I remember now that I had a dream about someone taking me to a dark scary place, in my destroyed world, to take off my face. I was screaming and begging them to stop this, but this person said:

"See you, Harley." And I went blind.

Anyway, I'm not Harley anymore, my name is Cooper in this world, "COOPER," I shout.

"Maybe."

"From tomorrow, you'll never bother me," I reply to my brain while drying the floor.

I read a lot of books just to understand who I am and what my mission is in this world, and today I'll start reading a book about the fifth universe and how this universe formed, so I grab *The Creator could be Created* by Allen Woolmstek.

I sit on the couch and open the book keenly.

"The unlimited universe begins with a limited big bang, the stars created from the dust in the space. Comparing the universe with dust leads to our belief about the city. A single human can create a whole world in his mind, and configure it in the real life too." Well, it sounds interesting, especially because the author believes in the big bang theory too.

After a half-hour, I decide that it's time to change the book and know more about how I got here to this multiverse, so I grab another book from my library called *Another Chance* by Martin Hewman. I think this one will do the trick.

The first chapter is named "What are We?" which I decide to start with, so I sit on the couch and start reading.

"When it happens that two persons are living in different universes but are so similar in personality, beliefs, thoughts, and age and they die at the same moment, they will exchange lives and only the best will continue living while the other will simply disappear," I read aloud.

"I really feel bad for the man who I exchanged lives with. Sorry for being better." And I start laughing.

"Do you really think that you are better?"

"At least I'm good enough to be alive, otherwise you and I would be nothing," I convince my talker.

Two hours of reading has passed, and I know a little more about my life here, and I know that I was so lucky the first time

I died, but this life I exchanged with would be my last chance to live a normal life before I become nothing after death, because I don't think the life-exchanging will work again. I also read about this Nopoly, which has been built for the people who don't want to deal with the evil in this universe and all those creepy creatures out there who are the enemy. And the warlocks who are living with the demons have chosen the wrong side; their spiritual beliefs make them think that the power of being a demon can beat all humanity; well they are wrong, totally wrong.

I'll admit that I like these two books more than the first book I read, what was its name . . .? Oh yeah, *The Start of being Extinct*; that book claims either humans or demons will be erased. For me, I won't stop the fight for our race.

I put my fancy clothes on to feel smooth, or maybe to make the ladies dance with me at the party I'm headed to.

"All the ladies will have no chance against this charm," I compliment myself smoothly.

"Shame on you."

I raise my head, giving up dealing with it, and make my way out.

*

While I'm walking, I hear the birds sing to me, and the green trees are calling me to sit under one of them to enjoy the view of the local park. The park is full of colorful roses, which it is banned to touch. I sit myself on the ground, but when I lie against the tree that I chose to sit under I get a feeling of coolness from the tree, which feels so weird. But I ignore that and start staring at the clear sky that is carrying the flying birds. Luckily, it's not common to face demons on holidays, which is perfect because the police station is closed on Saturday and Sunday.

After a few minutes I change my mind and go to the café to sit there instead. New Fox is my favorite café for having the best chai latte in the whole city. I sit out to drink my coffee in the fresh air while I see all these people who are walking in their fashionable clothes. Some of them walk alone, but most of them are couples or with the whole family, which is so cute. The most remarkable thing in the atmosphere is their smiles and laughs in this colorful city.

"Look at this lady who is sitting in front of you!" My talking brain interrupts my positive vibe.

"Beautiful! But no, no, no," I reply.

"You can't forget her, can you?"

"Her? No, I don't . . ." I raise my voice a little bit, but luckily enough no one pays attention except the lady my brain was talking about. She looks straight at me while she drinks her coffee before covering her lower half face with the newspaper she is reading.

It's the first time I've seen this lady in New Fox café. I don't know, but I feel something special about her. Maybe because she seems unhappy, unlike the others in this city. But anyway, I'll get to the bottom of this by any means necessary.

She finishes her cup, but she continues reading the newspaper with great concentration, and that provokes me to go and ask her what newspaper is this she is reading? Because, as I know, there are no newspapers on holidays! But as soon as I stand up to go and talk to her, she closes the newspaper and puts it in her little bag, walking away with her sad face.

I sit down again while my brain tells me to follow her and ask her if she is alright.

"No, there is no way to follow her, because she saw I intended to talk to her and she walked away immediately; maybe she doesn't want to talk with anyone."

"Maybe," my brain responds.

"I'll never listen to you again, stupid."

I finish my chai with regret for what I did before.

"I hate to be ignored . . ."

"I thought you just hate demons."

"And you," I add.

I decide to do something else to change my mood, so I opt to go to the movies to see something interesting.

On my way, I can see the circuses everywhere in the city and the boys laughing at the locked demons who are getting shocked by the electricity to dance and hop like crazed monkeys. Another group of demons are standing in a stupor, and the boys are trying to hit them with stones to win prizes. And in the corner, there are more demons going left, right, left, right to avoid the buckshot, which is only allowed for the adults.

"Congrats!" I shout to the one who gets ten demons in a row.

"What a noble act!" my brain comments sarcastically.

"Against the demons? Hell yeah!" I insist.

"He's doing it in front of kids!"

"It's normal here, like when we take a shower at the swimming pool. People are showering in front of their kids and others', and no one looks at each other there in a bad way; and . . . and the kids know that thing is right against the demons."

"What thing? Say it!"

"Shooting the damn demons, okay?" I shout so loud that someone looks at me with confusion at hearing me talk to myself.

"I get excited, haha." I pretend I am with the crowd who are shooting.

"What gives them the right to . . .?" I calm myself down and say:

"Because it's the right thing in this life."

"Thing?"

I will just ignore this freaking talker.

Now I'm buying some donuts with chocolate; this is something I adore.

"Shall you eat all this chocolate alone? That will not be healthy for you, will it?" A dainty voice comes from behind me; it is the lady I saw in New Fox café. I can feel my fast heartbeat up in my throat.

"Ahaha, yeah. I like chocolate. Do you want some?"

"I can buy it myself if I want to, thanks," she replies nicely. I try to play it smooth and confident.

"I mean, what do you like to eat on such a beautiful day as this?"

"Let's see, hmm. I'll take cotton candy, thanks," she orders from the shop.

"So, you like to color your teeth. Interesting!"

"Yeah, I like to make an art party in my mouth," she says, smiling. "I can't hold myself from asking you this: why were you staring on me in the café?"

"Oh, no, no! I was looking at something else. But regardless, looking at a beautiful lady like you doesn't mean someone deserves to be frowned upon, haha."

"Who was frowning? Me?!" she asks with a small laugh. "No, I was just focusing on the news in the newspaper."

"Yeah, and this is what I was looking at; I was about to ask you: do you read yesterday's newspaper? It will be old news if you read it today. Just wait till Monday and you will get all the news about today and tomorrow."

"So, what is the difference if I read yesterday's newspaper or Monday's one; aren't they always positive?" She takes her cotton candy.

"Wow, you remind me a lot of . . . Eh, never mind . . ." I stop before I get myself in trouble.

"Okay, plus it's not yesterday's newspaper," she says grinning.

"What was it?"

"News from the future, by me . . ."

"Oh, really? Are you a hex? You know it's illegal to work like this, haha." I pretend I am calm to hear more from her.

"No, I'm not. I bring this news from the tears that can open gates to any dimension in any period of time, and then I write all the information with what I think and believe about them."

"Haha, another illegal work. It's banned to trade in news if it's not from the government here; don't you know?"

"I don't sell them, I just read them to myself," she replies.

From the first moment I met this lady, I felt something change in me, and I don't know what is happening with my stomach now. But I'm sure that this lady is very different from the others.

"But what's the point of writing the events you see if you have already seen them? Unless you sell them secretly," I accuse.

"I'm not professional in dealing with the tears, yet, and I like to write because the new livers in Nopoly get some sort of amnesia."

"Amnesia?! I've never heard anything like this before," I say in a low voice. She looks at me saying:

"So, you are the newest here, I see . . ."

"What's your plan for today? Do you want, maybe, to go to watch a movie?" I try to change the subject, "and by the way, I'm John Cooper."

"Jolly Wood."

I give her a smile while we're shaking hands, and my eyes are staring at her. I blink quickly, wondering if she will accept the cinema suggestion . . . Such an embarrassing situation.

"No, thanks. I'm not a big fan of cinema." She gives me a nice smile.

I knew it, she isn't interested. And that accordion guy on the corner makes me feel even madder.

"I just like to visit the tears; do you want to go there someday?" she adds.

"Aah . . . yeah sure! It will be the first time for me and a new experience."

Jolly starts spinning the candy's stick before she says:

"Don't worry, I know that you're not from here."

I'm shocked, and silence takes over me.

"Don't worry, I'm a person of secrets, and I won't let anyone know about you," Jolly whispers, smiling. "And I know a lot of the different universes."

"How do you know all of this?"

"Did you forget the tears that I told you about?" Jolly looks at me, wondering.

"Ah, sure. Well I actually read about these tears in *WWIII in the Seventh Universe*. Hmm, let me remember the chapter's name, yeah it's 'The Reality is Insane.'"

Jolly raises her eyebrows, and then she asks:

"You are the one from the seventh universe, right?" And I nod yes before I say looking at the floor:

"The seventh universe, which is the lowest unadvanced universe according to the historian Roslyn Polman. I came here via the life exchange because, in my world, a horrible attack destroyed the cities and probably the whole planet." Then I look at Jolly continuing, "Do we need to make a promise not to tell anyone about our hidden parts?"

Jolly shakes her head. "I don't think we need promises that can be broken by the time, but we can trust each other instead. No one in the city knows about you and they won't. People here believe that there is something called life exchanging, but they don't know that someone can come here in this way, because if they did, they'd inform the government, and the government in turn would have the pleasure of inviting you to the laboratory; and you know what could happen there."

"You'll be the first one I trust in this universe. You know, I read that the tears are available only to a few visitors who work in the polity; you should be an important person in this city, aren't you?" I say looking at her humble outfit.

"Some people don't need to follow the rules, and we are an example of that," Jolly says, laughing.

"So now it's secret for secret, I like that . . ."

"Kind of." And then she puts on a serious face. "You mentioned the attack on your country; I haven't seen that attack and how it happened yet."

"We can visit the tears you've talked about? I have no idea how the tears work, and no book talks about it, so it would be nice to have a new experience with you, Ms. Jolly."

"Let's figure out what just happened in your poor world. And call me just Jolly. Let's go."

I nod while I'm thinking about using this device to see what happened to my family and discover many other things I've always thought about.

3- For the First Time

I'm shocked! Because today was a crazy day . . .

I was with Jolly all day. It all started when I was in New Fox and I met that lady. When we decided to go to visit the tears, I thought it would be a fantastic adventure, but it turned out not to be.

"Let me remember everything that happened and write the important events," I say while holding a pen intending to write:

"I asked Jolly if she wanted to ride the vehicle with me, but she turned it down and just continued walking.

'Don't you want to ride the vehicle? Okay then, just wait for me!' I said to her.

'Don't let the dust hit your face," Jolly responded, giving me a cold smile.

'Nice one; you have sense of humour. By the way, your sad voice gives me the feeling that you are not quite happy even though you're trying to cover the sadness you have with some smiles and laughs. What can possibly bother you other than damn demons?' I went silent for a moment before continuing, 'In the end you belong to this city, not like me, an . . .'

'Immigrant,' she completed my sentence.

'Yeah, an immigrant.'

'We are all immigrants somehow.' She was trying to be nice to me, but I showed her that I am satisfied in this life.

'But because I have only one life, I need to live my life having a good time as much as possible—'

'One life? Are you sure?' Jolly interrupted me.

'Yeah, because having a chance at another life exchange is quite impossible; don't you agree?'

'I don't think there is any woman who resembles me in all the universes.' Jolly looked at me sweetly.

'It's unfortunate, but you have to change your mood from time to time, you know; having a good time is required.' And, here, she turned her head down again, asking an unexpected question:

'Have you forgotten her?'

I got an instant headache when she threw that question at me.

'Who? H . . . How did you know that?'

'I'm just guessing because a man like you can't be single without a lover. Did you find another one to love in this universe?'

'What a smooth compliment, haha. No one compares to her, no one deserves my love after her. All the ladies I know here are dolls with a perfect body like carved wood meant for a one-night stand. But my love in the last life was a unique one, so I would never forget her.'

Honestly, I can't remember her face nor her name, but all I know is that I had strong feelings toward the one I loved in the seventh universe, and I loved her with all my heart.

'May I ask her name?'

I couldn't say that I forgot her name, because it would be so awkward.

'Jo . . . Joll, her name was Joll, and yeah it's a weird coincidence, right?' I was blaming my stupid head because I knew that she wouldn't believe what I said, but she should know that I was honest with my feelings especially because I expressed them with wet eyes.

'She had a nice name, and sorry for what happened to her.' Jolly tried to show me empathy by pretending to be nice.

'No problem, at least you smiled again when I told you her name. Now you tell me, are you married?' I asked her to avoid any other questions about my past, which I had forgotten most of.

'Take this first and get me some photos in this beautiful weather.' She gave me a camera that was in her handbag and continued, 'Be nice with the camera; it's not from here!'

'From one of the places you visit, right?' And she nodded yes.

'His name was Harley,' she said before I dropped the camera, which broke into many pieces, and I felt my pupils open wide when I remembered what the talker called me in the morning before meeting Jolly; what a weird coincidence!

'Sorry, I'll buy you a new one,' I said, while she was smiling again; a cold, calm smile.

'It's okay; it's just a piece of plastic. I have lost people who were more important to my broken heart. My husband is one of them, who is gone for almost one year.'

'Sorry to hear that,' I responded.

'It's okay . . .'

'I believe that we all have more than one life . . .'

I wondered, what if I was the one I exchanged lives with; would she be angry at me in that case? Would she exact revenge on me? Or maybe she would consider me as her lost husband; that was what was in my mind.

We continued walking in silence, while I was throwing a look at Jolly from time to time without letting her notice. She had soft brown short hair in an old-fashioned hairstyle, which was covered with a black hat, and big, beautiful hazel eyes. She was wearing a dress the like of which I hadn't seen before, so I said:

'Weird question, what is your style?'

'I dress up in eighteenth fashion because I like this style more than the nineteenth.'

'It's quite elegant,' I said, trying to be nice.

'Thanks. Nice costume, by the way. The person who chose it for you must be so elegant,' she said, smiling.

'Thanks for the compliment. I did, actually, because as I said I'm lonely here.'

'No, you're not. Joll is with you all the time, you know it already.' And then she hummed. I couldn't speak, so I just nodded while I was fighting the keep the tears in place.

While we were on our way, someone screamed:

'There are two there.'

They had escaped from the circus; that's what I understood. I wouldn't work in the police as a captain if I couldn't use a El-lasso and keep my composure when facing danger, so I took my electronic lasso to catch the two of them and let the Eliminators take them away from here.

One of the demons had a creepy face with big black nails. It was a fast one! I couldn't even catch it, and the other one is jumping from a place to another and had a scary visage too. The problem is that the fast one is distracting me. But I had an idea, which was throwing my water bottle and electrocuting the wet place to shock these freaks. Unfortunately, it didn't work with the running one, and suddenly the soldiers came from afar to catch them, but I wanted to finish these demons with my own hands so badly.

'Jolly, give me your water bottle, please! Mine is gone.'

'Why? What are you trying to do by throwing the bottles?'

'To shock them, or one of them at least!'

'Sorry, but there is no water inside it.'

I was ready to rock those demons with a real gun: my baby revolver.

Bang, bang, and a demon was down. I was looking at Jolly who was shaking in fear.

'Don't be scared, it is already dead.' I was playing the savior role.

While I was talking to Jolly the fast demon came so close to her, but I gave it a punch and one shot in the leg. Whenever there is danger, my adrenalin spikes in one second, so I used that to save Jolly's life, which was close to the end.

The soldiers came to thank me after they recognized that I was a captain, and a big vehicle drawn by two horses arrived. Four bearers showed up to take away these two nasty dead demons.

Jolly came to me slowly and asked about these people who she was seeing for the first time, or so she claimed.

'They are the Eliminators, and their job is to get rid of the demons they have caught or killed. You seem new here too. Aren't you?'

'Yes, that's right,' she said in fear. I tried to calm her down and just continue walking.

'You don't have to be violent like this, I guess,' Jolly said in a quiet, broken voice.

'Is it the first time you've seen something like this?' I try to change the mood.

'Yes. I work in the Accepting Section; I help the people who come from outside the city to be accepted here and join us. So, I save lives, but on the other hand, you kill lives.'

I stopped walking and looked directly into her eyes, saying:

'You are saving the humans, and I kill the damn nasty creepy demons, so if you feel sorry for them you better go to the doctor because you can't live here if you can't see the demons are the real enemy to us.' And I turned my face away from her.

'I do. I'm just against killing them when they don't harm anyone; you could just numb them and let them be taken away.'

'I guess you have the sight, but I bet that you don't have the insight. Didn't you see how that fast demon tried to take your head off?' I asked her, but Jolly started trembling in fear.

'I'm sorry for raising my voice; I'm really sorry for shouting at you.' But she kept walking without saying a word, and that made me feel sorrier for what I did.

'Look, a candy kiosk! They're making cotton candy made like a flower,' I say, attempting to make her forget what I did, but she didn't even look at me. I tried to come up with an idea but nothing came to mind; my talker brain didn't say a word, like it does any other time.

'I lied. I don't remember, I can't remember.' She looked at me as she said with a sad face:

'Lied? About what?'

'I can't remember everything from my past. I don't know why; and I don't remember what my wife's name was, nor my mom's name.' I felt that I needed to cry, but I couldn't.

She came and put her hand on my shoulder and said 'I forgive you,' and gave me a sweet smile.

'Let's continue, and thanks for that.'

'For the touch, or the smile?'

'For the forgiveness and kindness,' I explained to Jolly, who gave me a nod to go ahead.

After a while, we approached the Ceraton House. I could see all the energy generators coming out of the building and huge wires going in through the walls. We went in after showing our ID. The place is incredible on the inside and has many sections. Our goal was the details of the attack that happened in my universe.

'Sorry, you can't go in, sir and ma'am, because it's a special section, and it's government property.' I looked at the security guard with so much confusion, and then I looked back at Jolly who told me that she had visited the tears before. But I was trying to prove myself to Jolly.

'I'm a captain in the police, and I need to get some information from this tear.' I showed my job ID.

'Eh . . . sir, the machine is not stable and I'm afraid that—
'

'Don't worry, I have full responsibility for my entering.' I turned to Jolly, asking her, 'Would you risk your life with me, Jolly?' and she nodded yes with gleaming eyes.

Jolly typed into the machine all the information that the Space-Time Catalyst needed to be started, like the date, time, universe, and coordinates.

'I'm amazed at the amount of information you have.'

'I read a lot about it.' She gave me a smile and continued, 'Now let the fireworks begin!'

We sat on the chairs, putting a kind of glasses on our faces as protection before a huge tear tore the space, showing the other side of the world that was waiting for us. The first thing I felt was that I became lighter, and a flashlight blinded me before I opened my eyes and saw what was in front of me.

We were in the CIA building; I could see the sign on the walls. I stood up and started moving among a group of people who seemed uncomfortable, and they were all concentrating on their work. Jolly and I were like invisible ghosts, and nobody noticed us at all. The place was full of screens that watched the whole world. Suddenly, we heard one of the agents saying:

'From A5wc we have been hacked in Sandia, Lawrence, and Los Alamos; and we can't control the nuke missiles, repeat, we have been hacked and we have lost control of the missiles' launcher in three places in the United States, CAN ANYONE HEAR ME?' His head turned blood red, and his veins were throbbing.

I was frozen in my place with Jolly. Another one said:

‘Fifteen thousand missiles have been launched to a different part of the Earth! WHAT IS HAPPENING?!’

‘Holy moly, cut down the electricity on these three places, NOW! Keith, call the leaders and tell them we’ve been hacked! You roll the cam, and David, go and acquit the USA from the attack on the news. Say that we have been damned hacked!’

‘Yes, sir.’

‘FAST . . . MOVE!’

I would do anything to stop this hacking. I was seeing the end of our nation, our country, and our humanity in this world.

‘If any of these damn missiles bomb Russia, China, or even stupid North Korea, that means the nuclear war will begin because they will think that we, WE HAVE ATTACKED THEM IN THE FIRST PLACE, DAMNIT,’ one of the agents, who seemed to be the boss, shouted.

‘Bad news sir . . .’ someone said, and suddenly I felt confused and the world around me started to be disrupted like a glitchy hologram, and we came back to real life, sitting on the chairs again. I said:

‘WHAT THE? What happened?!’ We came back to the present at the wrong time! I needed to know what happened next! Did the statement work? Who could possibly hack the most protected agency in the world? How? And why? All my questions and more were left with no answer.

The first thing I saw was a man telling me I was lucky staying alive to this point.

‘This tear could tear both of you to a million pieces because it’s not stable, not at all. So please leave this section before I call the police,’ he said.

I was shocked, three times, that I couldn't tell him who I really was. The first shock was the occurrence in the Central Intelligence Agency, the second was when I was a couple of words away from getting an answer on what really happened, and the third was when I was close to being dead, to being shredded in my last life.

I felt dizzy, and I could barely move my hands with the feeling that I was carrying something very heavy on my shoulders. Jolly held me and said:

'Let's go home, Cooper.'

I leaned on her because I couldn't walk properly by myself. Then the man said, 'Do you need someone to pick you up in a vehicle?' I wanted to say yes please, but Jolly cut in and said:

'No, thanks.' And she turned to me, continuing, 'Come on, let's go.'

After leaving the building, I said to her:

'Why did you say that, it would be easier if we take the vehicle!'

'You are fine. A little dizziness is normal because we were in a tear; it's no joke to enter another dimension. And that man made you feel even worse by saying you were close to being dead,' she claimed.

'We *were* close to death; I was close to being just dust. It's easy for you to say that it's something normal because you used to visit these tears many times to get your damn news.' I was agitated.

Jolly turned to me and looked at me eye to eye, and whispered with a sharp tone:

‘Watch your language! Okay?’

‘I won’t accept that tone from anyone, you included,’ I said when I had calmed down a little bit.

‘You will, or I won’t tell you a secret.’ She gave me a sweet innocent look.

‘A secret!’ I replied, and I really wanted to laugh so badly, but I forced myself to remain the serious personality I had been up to that moment. Like, who cares about her secret now? Still, I wanted to be nice to her even though I didn’t have any idea why.

‘Tell me the damn secret,’ I said while walking.

‘Try again!’ and she turned her face to the other side.

‘Tell me the secret.’

‘Good luck next time.’ Jolly kept moving with her turned face.

‘FINE, tell me the secret please your majesty.’

‘Let me think first, hmm. Look, do you write a diary?’

‘No! Do I look like a beautiful princess with a pink hairband writing all my feelings to no one?’ I responded.

‘It doesn’t matter if you are a Viking warrior or a soft princess if you’re writing a diary; just try to write anything you want, and I promise you it will help you a lot,’ Jolly said.

‘Help me with what?’

‘Do so, and you will see yourself, trust me, Cooper.’ She looked sure about what she proposed.

I thought it was a silly idea to write a diary, but here I am writing it right now. That conversation made me forgot what just happened inside that tear. I stopped for a while, and then I asked Jolly:

'Did you see what I saw there?'

'I did,' she replied.

'There's something wrong; someone is lying!'

'Someone? How is that?'

'The book claimed that we had been attacked by the Huge Arch lands and the communist countries and that attack caused WWIII in my . . .' I stopped talking when I saw Jolly shaking her head no.

I felt my eyes would explode; I couldn't think or say anything, so we sat on a bench to restart my brain again because I was so confused.

After a while, I said in a low voice:

'Either Martin Hewman is lying or we were going crazy in that tear, because what we saw in that tear was totally different from what is written in the book; the book that everyone is reading in this city!'

'Maybe the book has some error. This Hewman is just a writer, and he could be right or wrong on some points,' Jolly suggested. I looked at her face, whispering:

'No! He is a philosopher and scientist who has been awarded in this city for writing that book after using the tears to visit my world with a permission from the government here!'

'Don't think about it now, and let's continue walking.'

I considered what I was supposed to do, and I decided to fix that lie somehow. This Hewman must be punished for what he wrote in that book because seeing is believing, and I saw something totally different from what he claimed. So, they'd need to check all his books that we have in this city and look into the information he had given in them.

'I will expose him in the discussion forum we will have in the First Lib today,' I announced.

Here came the worst part of my day, when Jolly started to feel dizzy, and she put her hand on her head saying:

'Please take me home, I don't feel good either, I can't even stand.'

'Where do you live? I will call an ambulance for you,' I said, but she held my arm.

'No, no, it's normal for me to feel this way, just take me to your home—if it's close—and let me take a rest there because I live on the other side of Nopoly.'

'Okay then. You can lean on my shoulder, and I'll take you to my place.'

No one offered to help, in fact, they were walking with a smile on their faces, because they thought she was drunk or something.

When we got home, Jolly let go my arm and said:

'Listen, you can't just demonstrate and say that the books have failures because they won't believe you; that will make all the books they have appear doubtful, think about it, Cooper . . .'

I was amazed that she had suddenly got better or had pretended to be sick.

'What was that?'

'What?' she replied.

‘For a couple minutes there you were dizzy and just needed to lie down. Do you usually feel better that fast?’ I asked doubtfully.

‘Do you want me to feel ill all the time? What do you mean?’ And she came close to me and gave me a hug, then I felt my eyes begin to close slowly until I couldn’t open them.

The last thing I heard was Jolly’s whispering:

‘Don’t get yourself into hot water,’ and I heard the door close.

I woke up after five hours with an extreme thirst, and the first thought I had in mind was to wonder if that lady was a professional thief, so I checked out everything in my home. It took me a half hour to ensure that nothing was stolen. Instead, I found a pink card telling me to write what had just happened to me today because I have amnesia caused by the exchanging! And a little notebook was beside it with a heart on it.”

It’s 1:17 a.m. now, and I’ve finished with my diary, which took me back to when I was young and writing stupid short stories. For now, I really need to sleep because I have to wake up again at 8 a.m. to go to the Temple of Science. I have so much to say to the public tomorrow; and that false Jolly will pay for what she did to me today, and I’ll show her who has amnesia when I throw her in the prison just like I threw that piece of paper, which was shaped like a stupid heart, in the garbage. I’m so, so angry at myself because it’s the first time I have been tricked in my entire life by a single woman.

4- A Week Before the Attack

I wake up like a drunk man who had a good night the night before, but the reality is that I had the weirdest day ever yesterday, and the thoughts inside my head spin and whirl.

"Just calm down," my talking brain comments when I hit the wall angrily.

"I DON'T WANT TO HEAR YOUR DAMN VOICE!" I freak out at my talker. "I was tricked by a mere woman!" I repeat out loud while punching the wall.

"That's why they say women are more intelligent . . ."

"Bullshit," I respond angrily, and I hit my head so hard trying to stop it talking, but my vision turns to green and purple, so I decide to calm down before I lose my mind.

I know, I'm probably sick and I need to go to the doctor, but something always tells me, in my dreams, that I shouldn't go to any doctor. I always see them with their white suits and black shoes chasing me in terrifying nightmares. Also, I don't want to reveal myself as an incomer from another universe, so I don't really know what I need to do with my talking brain other than hit it with my own fist.

I take a shower as usual before I go anywhere, and now I'm putting my clothes on to head to the Temple of Science. While leaving my home, I see Sebastian and his wife Sandra.

"Good morning, Mr. Cooper," Sebastian says with a wide smile.

"Good morning neighbors. Are you going to the Temple?" I pretend to be happy.

"Of course! Everyone should today. Let us be road companions," Sandra says. I give them a smile, accepting the offer because it will be better than talking to myself the whole way.

"Don't worry Areo, it's not so far away, buddy," I reassure my waiting horse, and we continue walking, leaving our horses in the stable.

"So, how are you, Mr. Cooper? Any new news?"

Any news! Of course, I have a lot of news to be honest, but I would never say a thing to them. They'd think I'm stupid to let a beautiful lady let me fall asleep.

"Everything is good, and nothing is new in my life. What about you guys?"

"Guess what, we're going to be parents and you will be an uncle soon, yaaay!" Sandra says cheerfully. I turn to Sandra saying:

"Wow, that's surprising; it's a good surprise. Congratulations!"

"Thanks man," Sebastian replies.

"When will the baby come to wake you so early, haha?"

"This is the best part actually, Mr Cooper. My wife doesn't like the small babies because they can be so annoying, and she wanted to escape the pain of birth, you know . . ."

"Yeah?" I reply for the excited Sebastian.

"So, we will have the child at five years old; imagine how the Birth-Away technology will make our lives better!"

"What?" I ask, and I come closer to Sebastian, whispering to him, "Sorry, but what is this?"

"It's okay man to talk about these things normally, haha; it's just science," Sebastian replies out loud, so I raise my voice, saying in a normal tone:

"Well then, tell me the process for this Birth-Way."

"Haha, it's Birth-Away; it's a very useful way to avoid the pain of birth and the easiest way to have a biological child at any age without ruining your life, haha," Sandra responds. I look at her, enquiring:

"May I ask how?!" Sandra takes a deep breath before starting to speak:

"First, we made love, me and my husband, as normal, heehee, and second, when the love mission was successful, we waited until that little baby came to the fetal stage . . ."

"Fatal? Haha." My sense of humor didn't save me with a better joke, but Sandra seems to like it.

"Haha, NO! The fetal stage is when the baby is twenty-two weeks old; then comes the third stage when they take that little tiny creature to take care of him in the baby care corporation."

"Him! How did you know his gender when that baby was only in the twenty-second week?"

Sebastian jumps in the conversation, saying:

"And that is the trick Mr. Cooper; the women's rights state that all women have the right to make their own choices with their bodies and what they have inside them. But fortunately, we have rights too in this city, HAHAHA." And he looks to his wife, still laughing.

"Honey, stop laughing so loud! Haha; that's so embarrassing."

“And what’s right that I have no clue about?” I stop walking and cross my arms.

“You should know this for the future, Mr. Cooper. Here we have the right to choose the gender for our children by telling the doctor who works at the Birth-Away corporation to change the genes that are responsible for determining the gender of the baby. That’s all I understood from the doctor,” Sebastian answers me before his wife cuts in.

“Let me continue the heavenly process, dear, away from men’s rights, haha. So that baby will be taken care of and will be raised fast to be any age for the parents in one year or something like that. Ours will be ready in fourteen months,” Sandra ends with a satisfied smile.

“I have a question, how would you know the child you will get is your biological child?” Both stop after I ask this question.

“What do you mean?! We trust the government here, and there is the DNA test; isn’t that enough proof?” Sandra says, frowning.

“Right, there is no doubt about it . . .” I try to end this conversation about this subject, which really scared me. Birth-Away!

After a couple of silent minutes, we get closer to the Temple, but Sandra breaks the silence by saying:

“So, honey, do you want to go for gambling after the cleansing?”

“With Connor and Teresa? Sure,” Sabastian answers his wife, who replies:

“And cocktail martinis.”

“Hell yeah, and what about you Mr. Cooper?”

“No, I have something very important to do in the Folk-Talk after the cleansing, can you guys stay for a while to listen to what I’ll say?” And they nod yes.

It feels so good to go into such a well-lit place as this Temple. I can see all the scientists’ pictures who all live here. Their wings, which look like old planes’ wings, are so recognizable with the shining stars at the top of their heads.

The smell here is so sweet, and the candles are lit all over the place, which makes the atmosphere so gorgeous. In the temple, everyone has his own seat with our names on the books that are placed on the seat tables, and every social level has a different tier in the Temple.

First, we stand and face a shining eye, which is always watching us here, to promise all the seven promises by saying:

“I promise the following: I’ll never go out as a citizen, never oppose the scientists because they are all wise, always be a good active person in Nopoly, be always faithful to this society, always keep in mind that we all love each other like a flock of goats, never let any demon free; I’ll either catch it or just shoot at till it dies, and never let anyone change my mind about this perfect life in Nopoly.”

“Now replace the *White Night Book* in front of you, close your eyes and sit where you place yourselves, please. Now, it’s the ‘Together’ song time,” a man with a white beard is encouraging.

Now we all sit with blinded eyes to hear the hymns and repeat just the first verse to feel like we are one voice against the dark closed minds; after that we’ll start to simply hear the rest of this beautiful song in our minds.

“*What are you looking for?*

Don't you know what's sure?

For what makes you alive

In this perfect life

***

Don't be worry, we live for the glory,

In a big small world, we are in this story

Read the book page by page,

Sing with me, like a bird in the cage

Breath wherever,

At least we're together

Yeah together, and forever,

No, no, nothing is better than to be together

***

We have to stay forever, and together

No, no, nothing is better, for now, and ever, my white pleasure

***

All these white noises though, clean all the dark choices for you

This the world we've created, we did all of that only for you

Forget all the wrongs you have done,

They all with the gods are gone,

Because the good ones sacrificed their souls to build these walls,

And they bless us, to live with science.

Close your eyes, and open the mind in silence

No one can run or hide from our guider

In the Temple, we will fly higher and higher

Together, and forever,

No, no, nothing is better

We will live, love, laugh forever and together

𝄞

Breath wherever,

We're always together,

And forever, nothing is better, than being together,

For now, and ever, my white pleasure

***

What you are looking for: is the Bezman faith for sure,

That will make you alive in this perfect life and form."

Suddenly, I see a blinding flash, and I become so paralyzed that I can't even shout. All I can do is feel myself drowning under dark water, but I'm still breathing; I'm not dead, yet!

Now I see a glowing door from afar, so I start to run without moving my body or my head; I move only my eyes. In the end, I manage to get out of this darkness and reach the blinding path to open my eyes and see all the people are smiling and hugging each other. A gentleman turns to me saying:

"Man, you have to be happy because we are alive and living in this heavenly city!" And he gives me a hug.

I can't remember anything; the only thing I remember is my work tomorrow and that I live in the city of civilized humans, Nopoly. And somehow, I feel so happy; I feel like I'm the luckiest man in this world to be here. That's right; everyone outside this city is either in danger or *is* the danger, and the others are dead. I'm so glad to be alive up to now, living the right way of life. I don't want to die before I live my whole life in peace doing whatever I like.

When I get out of the temple, I see the nice vibe that is coming from the dancing people with the classical music playing all over Nopoly.

"*Come to Happy Hill and pass by the west*

Give me the passion you have, and I'll give you my best

Let us drink for life and dance for the rest

Have some fun, so please don't come, but run to our fest

I know that you know me so please don't delay holding me, to your chest . . ."

And the music starts playing, making me dance while I'm walking. It's an unbelievable feeling with this beautiful song. I can't wait till I go to the fest to drink and dance with the ladies, but first, I need to go home and change the suit that I have on and dress in something else.

Before I know it, I'm home. I cast a look at the diary on my table, but I decide that it's not the time to figure out what's inside it now; I have to hurry because the ladies on the Happy Hill can't wait forever.

On my way out to my vehicle, I notice a lady standing in the corner and looking directly at me as if she knows me. I come close to her to ask her if she wants something from me or needs any help.

"Hello! Do you need any help?"

“Don’t you know how to gently light a cigarette for a lady?” she replies coldly.

“Oh sorry,” I say while grabbing my lighter to light her cigarette. I take out one as well to join her.

“Thanks, I’m Jollyn,” she says with a smile.

“Jollyn! I feel like I heard the name before!”

“Oh, really?” she replies.

“Yes, I guess that happened in one of my crazy dreams, haha,” I explain to her.

“And you are . . .?”

“Yeah, sorry, I’m John Cooper, nice to meet you.” And we shake hands. The lady is so gentle and worthy of companionship, so I ask her:

“So, what is your plan for today?”

“Nothing, what about you?”

“I’ll go to the fest on the Happy Hill. Are you coming?”

“And you expect me to be your companion?” she responds. I look directly into her eyes, saying:

“If you want to.”

“You are a kind gentleman,” Jollyn says with a wink.

“Thank you, and you look very well, but where is your vehicle?”

“Let us take the tram instead, please.”

She is beautiful, so I’m going to skip riding Areo for her sake, and we start walking to the waiting place to take the tram.

After getting into the tram and sitting, Jollyn looks at me, asking:

"You look amazing, where are you from?"

"Nopoly, I guess." I feel a bit scared by this question.

"Haha, no I mean originally; which universe are you from? I ask that because I'm new here."

And now everything becomes clearer.

"Well, I'm from here, the fifth advanced universe. What about you?" and I look at her scornfully. Jollyn nodes and looks at the floor, saying:

"I'm from the seventh one." She is from the same world I originally come from! No way of changing my initial claim.

"The seventh, hmm, so you came by life-exchanging." And Jollyn nods yes with sad eyes.

"Don't worry; I'm such a nice person and I'd never let anyone know about you as long as you're a good citizen." And she nods yes again with eyes on the tram's floor.

I feel like I'm proud even with faking all that; I have to be proud actually. Jollyn looks at me, saying:

"So, where is your family?" But I can't tell her the truth, for sure.

"I don't . . . I don't have one."

She looks at me with sorrow, saying:

"I lost mine in my previous life. I don't know if they are alive in their universe or probably in another."

"I'm sorry for what happenced . . ."

"Thanks for your empathy, but I've already found my love here," she says, smiling.

"That's great!"

"I also have a beautiful daughter," Jollyn adds.

"So, you are married! Why would you come with me then?! Does he know that you are with a random man?" I get a little bit emotional.

"We're sitting here as friends, and I'm just an associate to that festival; don't you remember? Plus, my man is open-minded; he also comes from the same world as me. We lived in a world that was infinitely free," she claims, and this makes sense because my world was actually so.

"No, it's just something in my manners, but it's really nice to hear that you have someone important in your life here. I lost my love because of a . . . a damn demon—"

"That's sad," Jollyn interrupts me emotionally. "My man works in the BioID company as a test sample, and this company conducts experiments on humans for a high salary," Jollyn explains with a voice colored by a deep sadness.

"The scientists here are surely doing well to develop humanity; I believe in their wisdom more than ours. And you know, I have a lot of respect for what your man is doing for this city." I just repeat what I have learned and been told.

Jollyn looks directly into my eyes saying:

"The issue is that our daughter is away from her dad most of the time and I'm little afraid for her—"

"And why do you leave her home alone today?" I interrupt her, and continue, "It's a holiday and you don't need to leave her to go out with strangers!" Jollyn gets confused and takes a while to respond:

"It's a holiday for my man too and he has to spend the day with his daughter. The holidays are my only free days, and that's why I'm with a stranger now."

What an abnormal family! It's not my business how they manage their relationship.

"I've got it. How old is your daughter?" I ask her, but she goes silent with eyes on the floor again. Did I say something wrong? "Sorry, you don't have to answer—"

"Five years old . . . I don't feel good, I'm sorry," she interrupts me.

The tram stops three stations before the Happy Hill, and I take Jollyn's hand, telling her to get off the tram, and she says:

"Don't you want to go to the Happy Hill?"

"Something inside of me was changing the first time we met, and . . . and it's become stronger in a short time. I feel like I know you! Do I?" I lose my patience to hold myself back, especially considering I've had weird feelings in my stomach since I saw this lady. Jollyn holds my hands and, looking directly into my eyes, says:

"Maybe, . . . ask yourself!" I redirect my eyes away from her.

"Listen, you have to go to your family because I'll have nothing to do with a married lady, okay?"

"I told you that my husband is an open-minded man." She lets go my hands, continuing, "And I told you that we are friends . . . or maybe more. Anyway, take this note but be careful and don't open it here in public; the effect of this notebook won't be available in that case." Jollyn walks away after this crazy speech, and all I can come up with is: "WHAT?!"

"Come say hi to little Lori, I have to go now. Bye!" Jollyn gives me a smile before she runs, leaving me shocked and confused about what just happened. I immediately get a painful headache, stopping me from chasing this lady. Lori! I know this name; I know someone with this name for sure. I . . . I'm just speechless . . .

BioID Logo

5- Unusual Things Happen Usually

It's 6:12 p.m. I just came home because I couldn't wait till I was home to open that note and see the effect that Jollyn claimed.

A picture on the first page is the first thing that I see; it shows a sad lady at the front and a person in the distance holding a little girl's hand. I can't recognize the person's features because he looks like a black silhouette, as does the girl. But I can clearly see the lady's face, which seems full of sorrow with closed eyes, and it has a cartoonish appearance. I turn the paper to see what's written: "Your amnesia is stopping you going further, so write what is happening with you on paper, and I promise you'll know me. And don't use the power of the one you exchanged lives with to find me; you'll not like the smell of the laboratories here."

That was what was written, as well as a picture of a heart. I'm really confused, shocked, and terrified of this crazy lady right now.

"How did she know that? HOW?!" I shout, full of negative thoughts and anger.

I double-check the picture, and I think that I come up with a meaning for it. I suspect the lady is that Jollyn, even though she doesn't look like her very much, and that person is her man, and obviously that girl is . . . what was her name? Lori, yes, the little Lori. I feel a shudder every time I think about this name, which I believe I've heard before.

"I'll prove that I don't have any problems with my memory when I visit my Doctor Diana tomorrow," I raise my voice angrily opening a new page to write,

I calm myself down and tell myself that I'm going to write about the events that happened to me today just to satisfy my curiosity about who she is and what I know about her. But first I need to relax myself and not let the curiosity change my mood. Plus, I'll treat it as an adventure that may break the monotony of this life.

I finish writing in the notebook after something like two hours, and I think I need some sleep so I can wake up early for work. But "Where is the effect of this note?!" I didn't open that thing as she said, but it still has no effect.

"Calm down! The lady was so confident with every single word she said," my talker brain starts its job.

"If that is the effect, then I'll burn this note. And why would you talk to me again?" I start shouting at myself like crazy, and it feels so good to get out the anger on someone or something that can't really reply to it.

"I'm your talker, your discussed head, so you can't run away from me forever."

"The only thing I hate in this dimension is you, but I have no one to shout at except you." I become a little bit calmer.

"Now listen, do you think that she is lying?"

"Maybe she is lying!" I answer my brain.

"Did she sound like a liar to you?"

"Why did she wait for me to talk to me in the first place?! I didn't know her before, that was just abnormal!"

“Maybe she had reasons to do so. You want to be an Explorer in the future, then you have to begin practicing and explore why she did that,” my brain plays the advisor role now.

“I promise that I will solve this mystery,” I end this conversation and put the note in the drawer with another note that I’ll not open now because I can barely keep my eyes open. I leave these books in the drawer and get to bed immediately to sleep, but my mind is planning what I’m going to do tomorrow, and . . .

*

At seven a.m. the alarm clock wakes me up, and I do my usual morning habits. As usual, I get ready to go out at 9 a.m. after drinking coffee on my balcony, taking a warm shower, and eating my breakfast.

Now I’m in my office looking at the city through the window. Nopoly is like a beautiful masterpiece. I take my eyes away from the window when there is a knock at the door.

“Come in!” I shout before the door gets opened by Marsen, who says:

“Good morning Mr. Cooper; Mr. David Krone needs to talk to you in his office.”

“Sure, I'm coming now,” I reply. Well, Chief Krone wants to see me! That scares me to be honest. Did Jollyn snitch on me? I should’ve found her as soon as I knew that she knew my reality. I have to be calm and memorize everything I read and learn to appear as an original Nopolyen. Let’s see what happens.

I arrive at the chief's office and wait for the guard to let me in. After two minutes waiting, the guard comes to tell me that Mr. Krone is waiting for me.

"Good morning sir, John Cooper is here."

"Hello, Mr. Cooper, have a seat please," he says in a cold deep voice.

"Yes sir."

Mr. Krone clasps his hands on the table and starts speaking:

"So, I see that you are a very good citizen of Nopoly, and so faithful to our nation with two hundred demons dead by your hands; that sounds promising."

"It's my pleasure to serve this city," I respond.

"As I see here in your profile, you are in the field of investigations. Are you happy in your position?"

"I'm always happy to serve this city sir," I repeat because I have nothing better to say in these stressful moments.

"You know, when I was a kid, I wanted to be an Explorer, but my body didn't help me to be accepted. I changed my goal but never changed my dream to be at a high level in my career, and that's why I'm here now. If I were accepted, I would be the goal you are focusing on," he says and looks at me scornfully. I don't like his look at all, but at least my muscles relax as soon as I suspect the reason for this invitation.

"The commander contacted me and told me that you have sent a message to him telling him that you're interested in being with ExA," Mr. Krone says while reclining in his chair.

"Right, sir."

"The Explore-Academic will open the door for people like you to be in the Explorer service, but the issue is that you will have a demotion to a corporal there. But anyway, I have no objection to this step," the chief says, smiling. I smile too, thanking him.

"You are going to do the acceptance test, and if you make it, drop by so I can congratulate you on the new position. But if you fail, you'll have to wait till you get lucky again to have work with the police. You should know that such an opportunity doesn't happen often, so don't waste it," Mr. Krone says with a flat expression.

"I'll do my best, sir!" I utter, so excited on the inside.

"Here we go, your name is on the list; they will send you a letter with details, good luck Mr. Cooper," the chief ends.

"Thank you, sir."

I get out of that fancy office, and I let my fantasy take me out of this city, as an Explorer. I can't wait till I do that test, and pass it of course.

I get back to my office, looking at it for the last time; hopefully, because I'll be an Explorer. That test takes up space in my mind, and every minute is like an hour waiting on my chair; I really want to go out to see the world outside Nopoly.

Mike comes in hurriedly after knocking on the door with a block of papers, saying:

"Mr. Cooper, there is a missing woman named Susan in the Accepting Section, unit B4, west Nopoly."

"You take care of this issue with your investigation team, and keep me informed of any further developments."

"Absolutely, sir," Mike replies and goes out of my office.

A missing issue! It's something unusual to happen here! But the lady will be found, and we'll know what happened to her because no one can hide from the guider who watches everything here.

It's time to say goodbye to my work today and get in my vehicle to visit Doctor Diana. It's very weird that my talking brain hasn't bothered me today; did I get rid of this sound inside my head? It'll be great if that is true.

I arrive at Diana's clinic in under five minutes and sit in the waiting room.

"Mr. Cooper, it's your turn, come in," the secretary says.

"Hello doctor, how are you," I ask Dr. Diana, who looks at me with her cold eyes, saying with a wide smile, "Well hello there, I'm good, what about you?"

"I'm still good," I respond.

"Still?! Tell me what happened?" I take a breath before starting the complaining:

"I don't know where I should start, but I believe there is something wrong with me. First, I have someone talking to me inside my head; I call it the talking brain or talker, and this thing keeps talking and arguing with me about everything like a crazy man."

"Does it have a special voice, or is it using yours?"

"It's not my voice, but a voice of someone I knew; a female one."

"Who?"

I start feeling confused, but I try to control my mind, answering:

"I don't know, and this is the problem."

"Did this voice tell you to go out of the city or to kill yourself?" Dr. Diana asks, wrinkling her brow.

"No!"

"That's good. Listen, Mr. Cooper, it's nothing to worry about; it's just your brain telling you stuff, and that could be good actually—"

"How can it be good when it's driving me crazy? It's asking me about my life, the city, and even my horse when I'm busy thinking about something else more important!" I interrupt her.

"I understand your feelings, but it's something normal and it happens to me, and that could happen to most of us; just calm yourself down and don't think about it as a problem. Let's say you have a companion to talk to and argue with unlimitedly," she says, giving me a small smile.

I look at the ground, considering her speech, and then I look at her, saying:

"Okay, I can practice coexisting with this situation, but I have another problem, and that's I might have amnesia; I'm not sure about this so I want to ask you how I can know if I have any sort of amnesia . . ."

"Let me just scan your brain and see what we have here." And Dr. Diana asks me to lie on the bed, and then she puts a scanning machine around my head.

"Oh, I see you are missing part of your memories, and it seems that you might not have been born here. I need to take you to our laboratory in this case!"

I freak out inside when I hear that and jump from the bed with a rising heart rate, saying hastily:

"No, no! Well, thank you for the scanning, but I see no need for that doctor because I really feel better now." And I head to the door adding, "Have a good day doctor."

"Thanks, you too. And don't forget the writing!" Dr. Diana says while I'm closing the clinic door in a hurry. I stop moving, looking back at Diana's face in shock, saying:

"Excuse me?!"

"Don't forget to write your name in the secretary's office before you go out," she says, smiling a cold smile.

"Yeah, absolutely," I reply, and I leave her clinic immediately to do so. I don't know what made me shocked there; I don't really know what just happened to me.

"It was so close, dumb!"

"Close enough to end you, Mr. Brain."

"With you, Mr. Cooper," my stupid brain responds.

*

Now, I'm finally home and so excited to see the letter that I took from my letterbox, which is from Explore-Academic. The test will be this Friday.

"What a Friday it will be!" I shout blissfully for getting this opportunity. The test will focus on physical strength and the shooting technique, which I'm very good at.

*

It's Tuesday, 10:32 a.m., and I see Mike coming to my office in a hurry.

"Good news, Mike?" I anticipate.

"Yes . . . no sir, the lady who disappeared has shown up again today at seven o'clock in her workplace, and she said that she hasn't disappeared and she's fine!"

"WHAT?! Who informed you of her disappearance then?" I ask him.

"The ID-pin showed that she was disappeared!" Mike says, looking at me as if I asked something stupid.

"Aah, it could be some problem in the pin; she has to fix this problem. Tell her to visit the ID-system office as soon as possible." I try to look like an expert.

"Sure, Mr. Cooper, but Dr. Diana has disappeared today!"

"Hold the hell on! What?! Send police portals directly to every possible place she could be in."

It's so weird for this to happen to the ID-pin because it's stuck inside the hand for every single one of us and granted for a hundred years, so how could it be damaged? Especially because the pin is connected to the nervous system, so it can't be stopped until the person is dead or the pin is taken out! I have all the information on the computer about Susan, and I can see that she has eight out of ten stars on her curriculum vitae, so I don't think she is a suspect citizen. Something is wrong with the pin, and I feel the same reason is behind Diana's disappearance.

To make the time go faster, I begin to read the book of law. I randomly open the book to read whatever page appears.

"Have a high level of glory by killing a low-class being slowly." This is a quote from the philosopher Charly Darsky.

“Catching a demon adds one hundred points to your citizen’s points, and that means a whole star for the social profile. The stars help the government know how good everyone is and who deserves to receive the concessions, like the financial support for example,” I read out loud.

I start reading the seven promises that we should follow and keep in mind at all times.

“They aren’t promises, but commandments,” the talker brain opens a debate.

“So what?”

“It’s like reading a radical religious book that you hate.”

“No, it’s not, it just promises to protect us as human beings in this world, and they are coming from a human being like me, not an imaginary superstitious being.” I get emotional.

“Who–”

“STOP!” I shout so that Marsen comes to see if I’m alright.

I don’t want to waste my time and energy with such arguments. This is the life of everyone who lives here in this universe and all universes: no god, no religion, but manners.

Doctor Diana

6- Something Impossible Leads to the Blue State

The time goes so fast these days, and I'm happy about that because today is the day. I have prepared the past two days for the test that I'm going to pass today for sure. At 12 p.m. I have to be standing in front of the commander doing my salute proudly.

"Are you ready?" my brain says.

"I have been waiting for this opportunity for a long time, so I'm pretty sure that I'm ready to be an Explorer and see the world outside this city without breaking the law; I know that I'll make it because nothing is impossible," I respond to it.

"I'm proud of you actually! Good luck!"

"Haha, for the first time, thank you."

I don't know what is going on with my brain; it's giving me positive vibes, so I'll try not to be harsh with myself today.

I dress up my costume, and I'm ready to go to the Hidden Arena where the test will be.

"It'll not take us more than ten minutes to get there, right Areo?" I say while getting in my vehicle.

Among the living city, I'm riding and seeing the happiness on the faces everywhere, but I guarantee that my happiness isn't comparable. I hear the people screaming from afar, and the crows are flying above that place; what is happening in the next street?!

"Shall I go to see what is happening?"

"You'll be late if you do!" my brain responds.

"If you tell me that, then I'll do the opposite. I'm still a police captain right now." I change my route to the spot where the people are running away from. Within just a few meters I see what is causing this chaos; a damn demon. The police are struggling to catch it, and just before I shoot it, one of the police officers shouts:

"We need that one alive!"

"Is it that important . . .?" I reply while grabbing my El-lasso to shock this demon as fast as possible so I can continue riding to the Hidden Arena. The problem is that this demon can disappear and attack from any unexpected place, so I come up with an idea. I pretend that I'm falling and freaking out with fear; that works. The demon attacks me after attacking one of the police officers, and just before it nails me, I hit that freak with the El-lasso. That is enough to get the demon electrocuted.

I'm leaving the place in a hurry, but I can hear the thanks from everywhere, which makes me feel proud of myself.

"You didn't need to waste your time with that one!"

"Can I hear your silence?" I reply to my brain, which continues, "You'll be late, for sure!"

"Areo, faster, faster! Come on buddy," I hit my horse's backside with the whip.

"I feel sorry for him—"

"Him? It's just a horse, when are you going to learn that?!" I interrupt my stupid brain.

Three minutes later, I arrive at the place; I hope the commander will not kick me out for being five minutes late.

I'm waiting in front of the huge gate to the arena after ringing the bell and saying my name and why I'm here.

"Sorry, you will have to wait," the security responds.

After a few minutes, the gate opens and I get in, in a hurry, with the security.

"John Cooper here sir, please accept my sincere apologies commander, but I had a problem on my way here . . ." I salute the commander.

"Hello Mr. Cooper; we know everything. Now come and join the competitors," the commander says, and I reply, "Yes sir."

I don't know any of them; they are all new faces to me, but I have to focus now on the test I'm still excited about.

"Welcome everyone. I'm Commander Jack Willson. As you all know this is the Hidden Arena, and the test will have five different levels; you will have to pass all these levels to be official Explorers, and remember you have signed that you are taking this test of your own free will," the commander clarifies in a raucous voice. We all shout at the same time, "Yes sir!"

A middle-aged man, who is on the right-hand side of the commander, takes a step forward saying:

"Hello everyone. I'm the manager of this test, and my name is Feller Rock. There are thirty-four people who will do the test. If any one of you fails, that person will leave the location immediately with a loss. All you have to do is carry out the commands without any objection. And for now, let's begin the first level of the test, which will be the Endurance. You must dress up in heavily armored clothes weighing fifty kilos, which will be distributed all over the clothes. You'll run all over the arena without stopping, then when the full circuit is completed, you'll move to the next stage; there you'll hold a gun and fire at the targets with full control. You have ten minutes to finish this, and the time starts now. Let's go, kidnappers."

Every single one of us, literally, stops and looks confused; this man called us kidnappers!

One of the participants in the test asks:

"Why are you calling us kid—"

In one second, even before the man completes his sentence, two men in fully armored uniform come from nowhere and take this guy away while he screams and begs to be forgiven.

The silence hangs over the place; all I can hear is my heartbeat. The roles were clear: we don't need to talk; we are just to carry out the commands, and that might be part of the test because what we are called doesn't matter; what really matters is the act.

The armored clothes are so heavy that I can barely put them on. After a long struggle, I start to run as fast as I can. The pressure on my body is so strong that I can't take a full regular breath, my heart is punching me from inside, and I feel so dizzy because of running with all the weight I'm carrying.

While I'm running, I feel like I'm losing the focus in my vision, so I shake my head to hopefully bring it back with heavy breathing.

Finally, I finish the cross with a swimming pool of sweat inside my clothes. I take a long breath before going to the target area.

It's the first time I feel I'm unable to carry a gun to shoot the targets in a tight time; that makes me nervous, really nervous. I try to hold the gun with all my strength, forgetting the weight of the clothes and remembering the reason why I'm here; discovering this world I'm living in. With one magazine, I hit all the targets, and I get down on the ground like jelly, relaxing myself with one and a half minutes left.

In the end, fewer than half of the competitors finish the first test. I'm thinking about the next one and how many of us will pass it in this case.

"Congratulations to all of you who passed the Endurance test. Take off the heavy armor to prepare yourselves for the next test, and better luck next time to the losers whose time has finished here and have to leave the place now," Mr. Rock decides, so the unlucky ones are leaving in sorrow right now.

One door is closing and another one is opening for us, showing a dark room, and some of us begin to move toward the opening door to satisfy their curiosity over what could be coming from that door.

Hastily, a group of demons has jumped from that dark spot, and the people who had enough curiosity to get close to that door have no faces and are transformed into ugly, terrifying demons who get shocked by the electricity with the other demons.

Amid all this horror, Mr. Rock says calmly:

"Don't do anything I haven't told you to do, even looking. Now your second test the Surviving Plan begins now; don't kill these demons, but arrest at least one of them using the cages which are above you."

I look up and see huge metal cages hanging on the massive ceiling, and I'm wondering how in the hell I'm supposed to get this cage down in the first place. At the same moment I'm thinking, two demons are coming at me with their scary faces; in fact they are the transformed ones. I begin to run as fast as possible without any plan in my head, and while I'm running two of the competitors are losing their human shapes and becoming demons, which makes me feel so disgusted. These demons have an ability to transform us into freaks like them! Well that's something new . . .

I can't kill these things, but they can take off my face, cut me into pieces, or make me an ugly demon like them in the best ways. It's just unfair, and it feels like I'm incapable when only one side must play roles and the other has full power to take your life. Why shouldn't we kill these scum?! They are demons, and they want to kill us so hard; I don't understand . . .

Now, I begin to think and plan while running from side to side to avoid the fate I would hate to end in.

"I have the power and the will to change my fate," I scream, encouraging myself.

"You can't change your fate." My brain is joining in to make the test extra hard.

"Yes, I can, and I'll prove it," I respond, realizing that there is a handle with gears on the wall.

The demons are right behind me; thankfully, they have no plan, instead they are just following me; nevertheless, if they catch me, I better be dead. I head to that handle and start pulling it, which drags the chain out of the wall. After pulling firmly and carefully, I free the chain to pull it or let it be dragged by the weight of the huge cage, which in turn moves that cage up and down. Now I have to let it be dragged carefully to avoid breaking it and harming anyone in the Arena, so I need to strike a balance between being a good chain holder and a terrified person who could be killed any time by these crazy creatures who are jumping, running, and screaming dreadfully. I have to keep my head on, and to do so I'm rotating myself, doing all sorts of evasive movements while holding the chain. It's so hard to think about all of that while using all the physical power I have.

Seeing the cage descending so slowly is burning me from the inside because I really want to finish this stage quickly before these creatures finish me. Just a few meters before the cage reaches the ground safely, a new demon joins the queue by sinking its nails into my left hand, which makes me bleed immediately; thanks to the adrenaline, I feel no pain. I hold the chain with my right hand, and suddenly the cage drags down, dragging me to the wall so fast, and when that happens, I hit the stone wall with my right shoulder so hardly, and the sound of the falling cage alerts me to open my eyes and forget the pain to save the rest of my body. I struggle to my feet looking at everyone else who is busy saving themselves. No one helps anyone; they don't even look to each other, and no one is here to save me, even the commander and that guy Rock are standing with cold faces looking at us dying . . .

"Oh . . . God . . ." I say while I'm falling apart. I think my head has been hit also.

"They are all dead according to Bezman methodology! Who are you calling?" My damn brain always chooses the worst time to speak to me.

"I need anyone to help me, anything," I reply.

"Use the chain!" it says. Right, the chain is heavy but I can carry it with one hand, and in the same second the two lovely demons come with open hands, but I don't think they are going to hug me.

I use the chain as a lasso and rotate it so fast that it would smash anyone who comes closer to me. I do this while getting closer to the cage, which is lying on its side on the ground with an open door; it's my opportunity to get at least one of these things inside. I start to run faster and faster toward that cage, and now I'm standing beside it throwing the chain on the ground to let them come to me and trap them in the cage. It works, actually, and both of them run toward me while the third has found another candidate to try to murder. As soon as they jump to get me, I get down on the ground, meaning they go inside, and with one hand I raise myself, throwing the end of the chain to use it to close the open cage's door; and I wrap the chain around the cage's bars to make it impossible to get out again.

Finally, I finish that test with a damaged hand and a bruised shoulder. I can't believe it; I was on the verge of dying in the worst possible way. My power has collapsed, so I get down on the ground, not caring if that jumper who sees my weakness comes at me to kill me; I can't move any part of my body in this moment. And surely that demon will come at me in a hurry, because I'm a sitting duck. But suddenly, all the demons have been electrocuted, and they all fall down at once.

"Congratulations to the last three who managed to stay alive; please join the rest of the winners at this stage," Mr. Rock says.

This is insane; we were twenty after the Endurance, and now just eight of us are still alive! The twelve who were murdered by the demons were people; they were human beings!

"Now every single one of you will have a quick health check before proceeding to the next test."

I'm so shocked that the nurse who is taking care of my energies asks:

"How is your psychological state?"

"Good . . . but what about the dead people?" I reply to the nurse, looking at her with my wide open eyes.

"They are dead. It's that simple. Don't forget that all of you have signed that you have full self-responsibility for everything that happens to you in the test, right Mr. Cooper?"

"Right . . ." And I look at the ground.

After a simple health check for the injured ones, including me, Mr. Rock comes to us again to tell us that the next test will start after a few minutes, and the commander himself will be the examiner. Now that'll be interesting for sure.

We get out to the arena again to continue the test, which starts when all of us are standing in a line, holding the guns, and facing so many seized and covered things with different colors and shapes; I think that they are demons for sure.

"From now on, I'm the one who will give you the orders because you are in the Obedience Test," Mr. Willson says.

"Yes commander," we all shout at once.

"Mr. Cooper, you are very smart and talented at shooting, and I really like your skills." Mr. Willson surprises me with his compliment, which I respond to with "Thank you sir."

"That's why you are going to start this test. Jason, bring the purple bag to Mr. Cooper!"

I look at the huge Jason bringing me this covered thing with great difficulty. I'll smash this demon and pass this easy obedience test.

"Mr. Cooper, take that purple bag off, and count to seven, then shoot at the head," the commander orders me, and I respond with "Yes sir."

A demon, with its scary face and bloody teeth, is under the bag just as I expected.

"In seven, Mr. Cooper."

"Yes sir!" I reply to the commander while I'm wondering if I can make it, or if this demon will get me before I count to five.

"One, two, three, four, five, six, seven." A bang hits the demon's head, immediately leaving it dead with the blood on my face because it was so close to getting me.

"Jason, bring the green bag to the front, and Mr. Cooper, take the bag off. Count to six and stab the demon with this knife!" Mr. Willson says roughly.

The covered one this time is a pregnant demon! This is the first time I've seen a pregnant demon, even though I know that the demons proliferate like us; but seeing that demon with a big fiery stomach is something new.

I'm done with this one while I'm thinking and ignoring its screaming and shouting; it's dead now.

"The black bag, now. I'll count to five and you smash the head with your fist!" Mr. Willson is excited.

The black bag was covering a tiny demon; it's a child demon! The commander has finished counting and is looking at me with his sharp eyes, telling me to do it now. I hold that captured little demon, which opens its mouth, showing me the sharp teeth it has. I get the black blood all over my face and my fist after smashing that little head.

"Nice work, Mr. Cooper. I'm so proud of you. You are two steps away from being a noble Explorer. Are you ready for the next step?" Mr. Willson demands, and I give the obvious response, "Absolutely, sir."

The commander gives me a smile, saying:

"Jason, the red one." And under that red bag is a lady with a little boy and a baby girl in her arms; and no one is seized. I can see the terrified mom covering her children's eyes with her arms, and her tears.

"Bring us the boy, and do whatever it takes to do so," the commander says with a cold serious face. I remember what just happened with that man who tried to talk without any permission, so I stop thinking logically in these moments. Anyway, it's just a normal order and I know the reason for it, which is to prove that I'm totally faithful, so I'm going to do it.

I approach the lady who looks scared, holding her children tight and close to her. So, I try to play the role of a nice person who just wants to obey the order, with a little smile; I hope it will work. But the lady is refusing to give me the boy, who in turn does not even look at me.

I turn to the commander, who is looking at me with his sharp eyes and cold face, waiting for me to bring the boy.

“Calm down! I’ll bring you the boy back, I promise. Just let me execute the order ma’am,” I ask so nicely, but she shakes her head with tears in her eyes.

“We don’t have all day, bring the boy now, Mr. Cooper!” the shout comes from the commander, so I drag the boy by the hand without looking at his face nor his mom’s, who is holding his other hand with her right hand (because the left one is busy carrying the baby). But my force is stronger than theirs, so I take the boy from the screaming mom.

“The last step, count to three and kill that mother!” I look at the commander, who looks serious, and Rock, who is nodding his head telling me to obey the commander’s order. It’s not a joke; that’s not a test of my loyalty, it’s a crime against humanity! But wait! Maybe the goal of this order is to test my humanity overall.

“Excuse me, sir, but I cannot do that?”

“Cooper! Kill that lady after counting to three! It’s an order.” Mr. Willson sounds so serious about it!

“Why?!” I wonder, feeling my heart beating in my head.

“Why! Because I order you Cooper,” the commander replies, full of anger.

I hold the Smith & Wesson gun with shacking hands and sweaty forehead. My brain jumps into this situation, saying:

“Do you really want to kill her?”

“It’s not your time,” I reply in the lowest voice possible.

“She is a human being! What are you thinking? Drop the gun!”

"SHUT UP," I scream at myself hysterically. I look around me, seeing the commander, Mr. Rock, and that terrified lady open their eyes wide, and they look shocked.

"Who are you talking to, you scum?" Mr. Willson asks angrily with red open-wide eyes.

"No sir. I'm sorry, but I have someone in my head, a . . . a talker, and . . . and I just . . . I'm sorry commander . . ."

"I don't care what you have in your damn head. For the last time, KILL THAT damn lady!"

"She is a human being . . ." I say in a barely audible, trembling voice with tears in my eyes.

"Speak loud and clear Cooper!"

"Commander, I won't kill this lady who is holding a baby in front of her child to be a damn Explorer. That's impossible, so I quit . . ."

"Congratulations, Mr. Cooper, because you have become the one who sacrifices himself to show the others what could happen when someone disobeys my orders. Jason and Harvey, take this former captain and apply the Blue State to him."

I'm confused because I don't understand what is going on, but I'll defend myself with the gun that I have.

"Put the gun down, the bullets are blank!" Rock says with a confident smile.

It's really blank; I thought he was lying but he's not. The gun does nothing when I shoot at these two huge guys who are now taking me to a tiny room, after getting hit in the head by a hard thick baton, while I'm hearing the commander shout at the others that I'm going to lose my old life, including my job as a captain in the police.

My hearing is not working, maybe because I'm deadly shocked, or maybe because I'm in a closed room full of medical tools and syringes. I don't know what is going to happen to me, but I have a bad feeling about all of this, especially that no one is answering my questions.

I keep shouting like crazy till my power falls apart and my eyes close.

7- Finally, I Know Who That Lady is

With a blue light above me, I open my eyes so hard; I have a headache and am seized on the bed. Dr. Diana comes with a weird smile.

"Doctor, help me please; I don't know what's going on here, please untie me. They are going crazy out there, please Dr. Diana."

"I've never thought that I'm going to do that with you."

"Do what, what do you mean?"

"We are going to clean all your memories."

"WHAT?! WHY?"

"Because you already have bad ones. In the end, you'll thank me for removing all these nasty things in your mind," she says, laughing.

"So, you admit that it's nasty what they are doing out there!"

"Yes, and that's why I'm here, to help you, former captain."

"That's inhumane to shoot an innocent person just to pass a damn test!"

"It was a blank bullet, Mr. Cooper, and you have failed the test. You have signed for all of this on papers; don't you remember?" she says while she is preparing to numb me for the surgery.

"I didn't read anything about this crap. Aaah! I'm stupid; I deserve that. I'm sorry . . ."

"Don't be, and stop crying! You'll have a totally new memory; is it not good?"

"No, I'm sorry for myself. I don't want to lose my memories, please!" I'm begging her, but she is just ignoring me. "What will I become without my memories? NOTHING! DAMN IT!"

Diana goes into another room to continue her work, but as soon as she enters here again, she falls down, and all I can see is her legs, which start to vanish in the darkness of the other room.

"Hello! Who is there?" But no one is answering. Instead another nurse shows up with a weird creepy smile.

"Who are you? What is happening? Where is the doctor?"

"Do you need that doctor who will remove your memory, or . . . maybe your life?"

"All I need is to get out of here."

"Got it! Let me just take off the track-pin," the nurse says while checking my head, and she continues, while throwing the pin away, "Are you ready to be free, but wanted?"

"I have nothing to lose, just untie me, please."

"Under one condition. Just follow me!"

"Deal!"

She unties me and looks me up and down like she's checking me out!

"Do we know each other?"

"Follow me!" she whispers.

I don't need to think about whether it's right to escape or not, because for them I'm just a traitor, so I'm done for them and probably dead. I'll run for my life I don't have other choices.

"Can you help me open this slot, Harley?"

"Excuse me ma'am, but my name is John, what can I call you by the way?" I say while helping her open the slot.

"You can call me The Mom."

"Oh, okay. Thanks, The Mom."

"Now give me a hand so I can get up to the ductwork to drag you up and escape out of this place."

After I get up to the ductwork, the lady drags the slot using a rope to close it perfectly, and I start following this Mom.

"Why are you helping me? How did you even know where I was? And how did you get in that place with all the security in it?"

"I'll answer all your questions later, I promise. We have to hurry up, Harley."

"This ductwork is so tight for me, The Daughter." As soon as I say that, she stops crawling, puts her head down, and starts shaking her shoulder like she is giggling.

"Is it a good time for laughing?"

"The daughter is saving her dad; that's funny. Let us continue."

"I'm not your . . . Oh my God; let's go."

After a half hour of turning right and left, creeping in the ductworks, The Mom stops and says:

"Well, it's time to get out . . ."

"Do you mean Nopoly?!"

"Are you that excited? No, first we are going out of this tiny place," and she points to the ductwork before opening a little door and getting out of the ductwork; and I follow her jumping on an empty place from any kind of human being.

"And then we'll go out of this enormous place," pointing to the city, in which nothing seems normal at all. More police patrols walk around, and the crows hover everywhere.

"Can you trust me with your life?"

"Can I at least know your real name?"

"Joll."

"Huh?! Aah . . . Nice name!"

"You seem surprised."

"This name reminds me of someone crazy. It's just similar; maybe it's just a coincidence!"

"I don't think so . . ." she says and gives me a weird mask which she had in her bag. It's a human face!

"What in the hell is this?!"

"Let me put it on your face; it's a mask to cover your beauty."

"That was a good flatter, but unfortunately it's not going to work with me," I reply, struggling to say it properly while she's sticking that thing on my face.

"What do we have to do now?"

"Act normally, keep smiling, and follow me!" she says, and she puts a new one on her face too.

I look doubtful while I'm looking at her with her new face. She comes to me and puts her hand on my shoulder saying:

"I've told you my name, don't you remember?"

I nod, telling her that I'm trusting her, and we start moving. I see the beauty of Nopoly with its happy people, the vehicles, and the trams. But more crows flying in the sky.

"Joll, where is the destination?"

"Somewhere they can't take your head off with your memories. Just stay calm and . . ." Joll stops talking when a police officer comes with a crow, which starts to stare at me and Joll.

"Good afternoon sir and ma'am, but we are looking for two demons that are hiding in Nopoly; if you see one of these two or both, please call us directly," and he gives us a photo. I look at the photo and one of these two wanted demons is me! Cooper become a demon now! That's just crazy! But thanks to the new faces we have, the officer couldn't identify us.

"Sure, sir," says Joll with a smile, and she holds my hand telling me we have to go.

"Look Harley, I—"

"John! My name is John Cooper, please!" That name belonged to me when I was in my last life, and I don't like to be called that name anymore. I don't want to ask her how she knew my previous name; all I want now is to stay alive somehow.

"With this new face, you are Harley now!" Joll says insistently.

"Fine! But, are you from the seventh too?"

"I am. Now look, I'll take you to the Accepting Section where I work, and from there we are going to escape from this nightmare."

"Wait, what?! So, we are going out to the demons? Are you trying to kill us?"

"With me, there's no demon will touch you; I promise."

"Ooh, are you a demon-terrifier or maybe a nun? Because if you are, I'm an atheist, and I, personally, don't believe in either of these—"

"But you believe that there are demons! Anyway, I told you my name, and I think you're a man of your word! And no, I'm not a nun, but a mom." I consider her words, which make sense, but I come up with this question:

"Mom to whom?"

"To a beautiful girl . . ."

"Is she alive?"

"You'll have to ask your Explorer Army!"

I stop walking and start staring at the ground. It takes a while before I come back to this world again.

"You need to tell me everything in detail after we get the hell out of here, okay?"

"That's the whole point of saving you from here!"

A million thoughts and scenarios are playing inside my head now, so I stop thinking about who this Joll is, and all I need to know is the truth and the reality of this world.

Now, we are in one of the Accepting Section's areas. I stop in my tracks outside the building as Joll asked me before she goes inside. A lady comes to me with a mask on her mouth:

"Mr. Harley, it's me Jollyn, do you remember me?"

"The lady who left me at the tram station?"

"And gave you a notebook; it's me." I am shocked to hear her say that. Why is she appearing here and now?!

"Where is Joll then?" I ask her, looking left and right.

"I've taken the N and the Y from her name."

"Wait, what? Why?!"

"Yes exactly, Y. Do you think that we all have our real faces here?"

"What do you mean?" I ask, crossing my arms and wrinkling my brow.

"The Nopolyens have so many faces in this city; even I, I have many faces."

"Why?"

"I do to save you from here, and no more questions now; we have to move now."

I stop walking, looking at the ground, and then I look at this lady who I don't know what to call.

"I need to know everything." I tell her this with my head to the ground and eyes on her.

"You'll also see my real face soon; let's go."

I have no clue what this lady means, who she really is, or what is about to happen next; all I know is that I'm wanted and following a beautiful lady who wants to save the rest of my life.

We are inside the Accepting building, and this Joll or Jolly—I don't really know—shows her ID everywhere we go into. She's telling them that I'm her nursing assistant, and she will be the one who will lead me in the workplace.

In the end, we come to a place that has so many wires, screens, and computers but is empty of people. It's just me and this lady in this cold room.

"Are you ready to go out?" she asks me, and I nod yes.

"You don't need that mask anymore so take it off!" she says, locking the door. It feels so uncomfortable right now with that tone she has adopted.

Jollyn picks up two gas masks and a suit, asking me to put one mask and the suit on, and she turns the handle down and pushes a red button in a hurry.

"Wha . . . what are you doing?" I ask her while putting the mask on.

She is too busy to answer me, but my talker begins speaking:

"Who am I? Or who is she? It'll be better if you ask who you are!"

"Wait, I think I'm going crazy!" I shout, looking around me.

"Seeing is believing, and this is the biggest lie you are living."

"Why . . . I . . . ?!"

"Is it real what you see? Have you considered about things you can't see? Is thinking confined to vision?"

"I heard you twice! I'm going crazy! Please stop!"

"I'm your soulmate, your savior, I'm your love Jollya."

"What?! How?! Is . . . is that really you?! You were talking to me all the time through my head! How? When did you come here?"

"What do you mean by 'here'?"

"I thought you were dead, in the seventh universe. Can I see your real face to believe you?"

"There is no seventh universe nor fifth. This is the same universe we know; and I'll show you that soon," she says, smiling.

After a few seconds, the gate starts to open and that lady seems so busy getting out stuff from her black bag. Suddenly, the alarms are activated in the building, and we can hear the heavy steps coming closer and closer to us.

"Now, it's time to open your eyes to the reality," she says, starting to take her face off slowly, showing me her real face this time. I can see her face is bleeding dark blood, and just then I realize that it's not a human face but a demon one with the fiery eyes, and big teeth; it's a smart demon that used a human face to drag me all the way to this place. She puts the gas mask on again over her nasty face.

What a stupid, hopeless man I am. What a shame I got to really work with a demon. What a pathetic situation I put myself in to let a damn demon play with me like this. I feel dizzy and nauseous with some blurriness in my vision. My legs can't hold me anymore, and my arms disobey my orders; I just sit on the ground paralyzed by the shock. My body is doing as I did before with the commander by disobeying the order. Is it karma?

"You win; now tell me, what do you want from me? Killing me? Is it the most ambitious job you'll ever make?"

"I'm sorry, I didn't mean to scare you with my real face; I want you to calm your dismay because the reality is terrifying, baby."

"I SAID WHAT DO YOU WANT FROM ME?" I feel like I have no balance, and my brain stops. "I don't understand . . . I thought you were here to help me with goodwill toward me; I never thought that you'd be a demon. What a dumbass!"

"I'm here to save you from Eeewskesh Wasch . . ." I start to hear that noise that usually comes from the demons. Now I get it, and I think she gets my feeling toward her because she sees the disappointment in my eyes caused by her betrayal and deception. But then I remember what I did in the Hidden Arena. Is it karma?

"Why did I trust you. WHY?!" I scream, trying to punch the floor with a heavy hand as if I want to take my revenge on anyone or anything.

The gate is open now, showing a dark, depressing world, and the winds starts getting inside the room; and that demon picks up a gun.

"What is that? What are you trying to do?"

The demon is still ignoring me, and it shoots a red flare toward the outside.

After a few minutes, a band of terrifying creatures that also have gas masks on come toward me from outside, which wakes up my brain to this nightmare that is starting to become real.

"HELP! Can anyone help me? I'm . . . I'm locked in with . . . six demons. Come in! Hurry up because there are more coming!" I shout hysterically.

She sounds so scary and creepy while she is communicating with the other demons. Wait, it's not she, it's a damn demon.

A group of demons comes like crazy toward me so fast, and they look so wild. So I prepare to defend myself, but I can still feel the dizziness, and I can barely stand up; I'm struggling to balance myself.

While I'm walking to the door, which has recently been punched and pushed from the other side of the room by the soldiers to smash the lock, I can feel my hands are shaking with my legs, but just before I reach the door, a hand drags me by my shoulder, and my end seems close. Three . . . four demons come closer; one is holding my left arm, one is on my right hand, one is tying my legs with its hand, and one is behind me. They are all trying to hold me back from moving, but I'm not going to let them control me because I'm the master here, and they are all just freaks and deserve to die in the worst possible way. But my strength lets me down this time and for the first time.

I know that my life is done this time, especially when one of these freaks, which is the smart one, comes closer to me with its disgusting eyes, and it puts its filthy claws on my face after removing the mask; and what a pain I get when she takes my real face off! My eyesight turns glitchy while I'm hearing a glitchy noise, before I become blind, seeing only a vast white. And something has been put around my moving head.

That's what I was afraid to face, and I'm facing it now when my face has been taken off, and I start to bleed, scream, and cry for my life. I beg them to leave or let me live just one more minute, but it doesn't seem that I'll be able to live anymore. All because of my stupid choices.

When my vision gets a little clearer, I look at my face, which is in the demons' hands, for the last time; I deserve all of that. Now I've lost all the feeling, and all I feel is I'm being held, and all I hear is words like: "open up . . . hurry up . . . hold him up!"

I start seeing double vision of so many people moving in front of my half-closed eyes; and I get laid down on a bed or something. I feel my body shaking; I believe they are taking me to the outside now.

For the first time, I see the dark fiery sky behind a glassy mask. A face covered with a gas mask shows up, shouting:

"I'm not going to let them take you away from me again baby."

Now, I really know who that lady is; this lady . . . It's . . .

"They've opened the door, hurry up guys, come on!" someone shouts.

I feel like I'm taken so fast that my body starts to jump on the bed. But the last jump comes with the sound of a bomb that gets me out of the bed to the hard ground.

The shooting starts from the inside to the outside, so I try covering myself with the fallen bed, but something grabs my leg and drags me back into the room. I can tell it's the Nopoly government's hand; it's reaching me now.

My vision starts to clear, and I wish it wouldn't because now I can see her crying eyes. It's her; I'm not dreaming because there is no way to see a dream that the government is taking someone from his wife in this harsh way.

I've been taken away, leaving her with all her tears and sadness, calling me with a loud broken voice: "Harley!"

The gate starts to close, and Jollya is on the other side kept from reaching me, not because of the open fire on them, but by the other outsider.

The fire doesn't stop until the gate is totally closed, blocking a hand stretching toward me telling me to keep holding it, but it's too late and so far away.

8- Mission Complete

"Nooooo!" I scream while I'm dropping from on high into the darkness, which leads me to a shining little gate; then, I wake up with a red light in a tiny space that has dungeon bars. Surely I'm in prison, now, sitting and seized in a cold place like this.

"First disobeying the commander's order, and then dealing with demons; what punishment do you deserve, Mr. Cooper?" someone standing beside Dr. Diana says; he looks like another stupid doctor.

"My name is Harley . . ."

"Demons' effect . . . I know how to fix him," Dr. Diana says calmly before leaving the room.

"So, you've started to recover your memory, I see . . ."

"I'm dead; I know that, but I gotta tell you that I've never betrayed Nopoly, I swear."

"You did when you worked with that demon."

"Sir, they're not demons out there; I've seen them. They are human—"

"Shut it!" the doctor interrupts me before continuing, "As I see, you've got back your memory somehow, and I don't have any clue how, but it seems someone has intervened in the process because that has never happened with any of the Nopolyens." After this crazy speech, he turns to me saying:

"Oh sorry, my name is Dr. Stephen Harris."

"Where am I? What just happened?"

"You can clearly see that you are in the safety of Nopoly, and what just happened to who? Do you mean your faithful demon friend?"

"She isn't my friend, I don't even know what she is, a normal human being or a freaking demon . . ." I say to avoid more questions about her.

"You've just said there are no demons! Come on Cooper, or maybe Harley . . ."

"I swear I didn't work with her; all I know is that she wanted to . . . to take me . . ."

"She almost did. Look, we need to know who the hell she is and how she got inside Nopoly," this mad doctor says, looking at me with his creepy gray eyes.

"I have no clue. I just saw her with a human's look and then she became a demon I really hate to see . . ." I know that I'm lying . . . I know.

"You know it's hard to believe what you can't see. Anyway, if you don't want to talk to us about her, I'm afraid that I'm going to let your brain speak instead but that will destroy your nervous system; so I'm going to be nice with you and give you time to change your mind and talk in a normal way."

"But I swear, I don't—"

"Hush, you need to clear your mind now till tomorrow. You'll not lose anything if you cooperate with us, think about it!"

That crazy doctor just leaves, locking the prison door after turning off the light in the dungeon.

I'm seized, can't see or hear anything, and I feel the cold is getting inside my bones. At least they didn't take away my feelings; they can't do that! No one can steal that from me as long as my heart is still beating.

At this moment, I feel tired, but it's nothing for a dead man who is waiting for his fate.

The bright side of being in a dark place like this is I can cry without showing that I'm weak. I'm crying for what I saw today, for what I missed, and for what I believe I had before this day.

*

"Cooper, wake up! You are going out."

I wake up with dismay saying:

"Field execution?"

The officer doesn't answer but looks at me coldly, and he takes my arm to move me to my clear end. My legs are shaking with dread; I can't think of anything but not dying.

"Don't move by yourself or you'll get electroshock that will make you paralyzed!" he warns me. I become blind after hearing "B20C" from him.

"I cannot see anything!"

"Because of the blinding code, now let's move!" he says, leading me by the chain he is holding; I become a loyal dog after being a captain, what an irony. I feel servile and unable to do a thing.

"After being a captain in the police, I became a traitor. I deserve this handling because I refused to kill a human being like you and me!" I try to appeal to what is left of the humanity in him, and he stops moving. I feel a hand on my shoulder, telling me that the owner of the hand can do nothing but sympathize with me . . .

"I'm sorry, this is the order; just keep moving," he says sadly, and we continue walking in a place that has warmer air and feels close.

After a while, we stop and the police officer says:

"I'm going to make you able to see again. C20C."

I can clearly see a place like a blocked alley, and the officer closes the iron door that leads to this place, locking it.

"You'll not tell us who that demon was, right?" he asks.

"No!"

"It was an honor to be with you sir; love you . . ." And he picks up the weapon and a bullet is shot while I'm closing my eyes. I don't know where I've been shot, but it feels like my soul comes out of my face, because I get so much pain in my face while I'm becoming blind. It's the last minute for me here. The first thing I can see is my wife's eyes, which are looking at me with fallen tears; no pain compares with this thing. Death isn't scary, but what is after death is pretty scary.

My vision becomes clearer, and with a little focus, I see a covered face with a kind of masquerade mask with black wires on the face and all over her suit.

"Am I dead or alive?"

"Haha, I didn't test the death yet . . ." his voice becomes a bit weird and with a smile, the mask is taken off, showing me the beautiful, lovely face of my wife.

"I don't believe my eyes! Is that you Jollya?!"

"Yes, it is!" she says, jumping on me and hugging me while my shock and the dizziness stop me from making any movement but letting the tears run on her shoulder.

"We better get out of here! And listen, everything you'll see from now is the reality, okay baby?"

I nod while I'm looking around me, and all I see is iron everywhere.

Suddenly, a high-pitched sound comes from above, so I look up to figure out what it is, but all I see is huge lighting screens in the sky.

"What is that?!"

"Calm down; it's the sound of freedom . . ." she says, smiling.

"Freedom?!"

The sound comes out again with a higher tone, like it's getting closer and closer, and it ends with an earthquake that shakes us so hard, and a blinding red light shows up, so I try to protect my eyes by covering the red light with my hand. It looks like a huge mech that have an iron owl face! How the hell are we going to escape from it now?!

Jollya seems stressed, and she comes in a hurry to untie me.

"A bit late, but thank you," I say, giving her a cheerful smile and looking back to that mech.

"Don't worry, baby; I'm going to protect you with everything I have." But the appearance of an iron owl's face interrupts this emotional moment.

"Put these on and let's go," she says, giving me a gas mask and a suit like the one she is putting on.

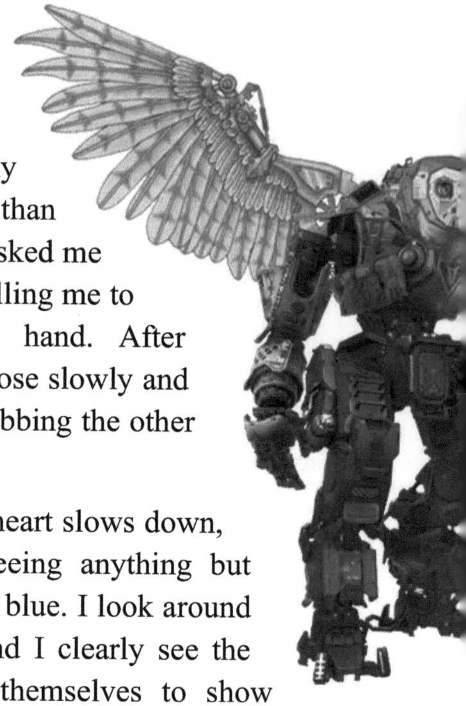

I'm so confused, but both my fear and happiness are bigger than my curiosity, so I do what she asked me to do, and she holds my hand telling me to climb on that mech's metal hand. After grabbing the hand, it starts to close slowly and gently to cover me. Jollya is grabbing the other hand as well.

Suddenly we rise, and my heart slows down, which is blinding me from seeing anything but Nopoly, which is colored a cold blue. I look around me with a little more focus, and I clearly see the bronze statues start breaking themselves to show flying objects with wings. They look like the one that is carrying us; and they are flying so fast toward us!

All I hear is the wings hitting the wind, the sound of the alarms in the city below us, and the fire coming from everywhere.

"THESE MECHS ARE SHOOTING AT US!" I shout with the taste of adrenaline in my mouth.

"We are getting out of here!" she replies.

A sound of smashing breaks my fear, and it feels like my heart has stopped. I think this thing which is carrying us has been hit and we are going to be shot down, but when I look down, I see that we are still floating in the air; and we get out of Nopoly. That smash caused the collapse of the huge screens, which are placed above the Nopolyens like barrier that is covering the whole city, leaving a gap in these screens. It seems like some crashes show us the reality, and now, for the first time, I see the real colors of this world. I see the red and gray sky, the destruction everywhere, the purple lightning, and the fires devouring large parts of America.

While we are hanging in the air, I look at Jollya puzzled with so many questions in my eyes, but I bet that she can't see all of these questions under the gas mask. All these thoughts fade away when I feel like we have been hit, and the owl starts to swing and fly unsteadily. At this moment I feel we have been shot down because we stop levitating, and slowly, we realize this huge machine can't hold us in the air anymore, so we need to jump off it. The guy who was controlling the owl gets out and says:

"YOU HAVE TO JUMP NOW!"

Jump?! I don't have any parachute!

"What are we going to do without parachutes?!" I shout to Jollya.

"I have one, so we'll have to jump at the same time to land together."

"Alright."

"Free yourself from the Plonster's hand and jump toward me. I'm going to jump with you too."

"Sounds crazy!"

I'm now trying to get out of these huge metal fingers of this damn mech, but it doesn't work; it's so hard to handle this in the air in such a rush.

"Jump, Jollya. JUMP!"

“We jump together!”

“I can’t. I’m stuck here.”

I feel like I’m going to land with this huge mass of iron and we are going to be crushed together. It’s good that didn’t happen with my lovely Jollya.

“Listen, Jollya, it seems I’m stuck in these damn fingers. Don’t wait for me. Please jump! Don’t . . . don’t wait for me.”

“I’ve never thought about leaving you before, and I’m not going to let a piece of metal separate us now. We’ll jump together! You can do it honey; come on.”

I hear the insistence in her voice and that empowers me, so there is no time to waste this magical feeling that I got from Jollya.

I’m trying with all my power to free myself, but my strength isn’t helping me. I’m giving it one try, two, three, and many times, but I’m stuck still.

The ground is getting closer every moment that goes by. I’m about to give up, but a strong sudden shake makes my body hit the metal fingers so hard that they start moving finally.

With the force of the wind, I realize that I’m flying through the atmosphere. I’m free now, but I’m falling at the same time. But where is Jollya?!

“Jollya! Where are you honey?!” I look up, and from above, she pushes herself toward me, stretching her hand to me.

“We need to get closer!” And she holds her limbs to her body to reduce the speed of falling and reach me before we hit the ground, which seems a couple of hundred meters away from us. And, finally, Jollya’s hands reach mine while I’m tumbling through the atmosphere, and the whole of Jollya's body is hugging me now.

"I catch you, my love. Now it's your turn to catch me," she says, wrapping her leg around my body, and I hug Jollya's abdomen, telling her:

"You are my guardian angel." I feel her smile without seeing it, as I feel the ground getting closer, and while I'm thinking, a shock shakes us and pulls us upward, and fortunately that isn't because we've hit the ground but because the parachute is open now. But we will still land faster than we are supposed to because we are two on just one parachute.

"We're not going to make it. Let me land normally, please Jollya!" I say and my hands leave her body, but she is shaking her head while she's holding me tighter with her legs.

"No way; we'll land together, dead or alive." She says this with a strong, powerful tone that makes my whole body shudder. And just before I catch a glimpse at the ground, I feel that I hit something, so I freeze automatically because I think I've hit the ground and my bones have smashed to pieces. That doubt seems logical, especially when I see myself get inside the darkness, leaving the light behind me and sharing the pain with every part of my body. Is this death? Is it really the end of me, here and now? What about Jollya? I hope that she survived . . . Wait! Why do I see the light again?!

While I'm thinking about how to escape from sinking into death, I float, suddenly on dark water.

"If I'd known that you'd forgotten how to swim and float, I wouldn't have landed on this lake and would've landed on the ground instead, no matter how many pieces we'll turn into, ahaha."

"Jollya! Are we alive?! Holy Heaven!"

"Yes, we are, and you are free my love, so mission complete . . .

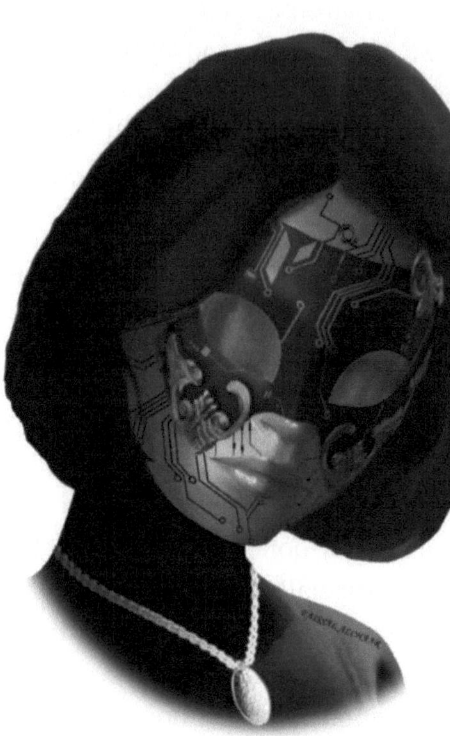

Jollya with VI

II. Outside Nopoly

9- The VI

After the biggest escape I've ever done in my entire life, I'm thinking what's next?

"I don't know if all of this is real, but anyway, I'm so glad to see you in this universe, honey."

"I'm so glad to save you," Jollya says and she hugs me; I can feel her warm, lovely heart, regardless of whether we have suits on or not.

"I need to know several things from you, and I really want explanations for what happened and what we are going to do next . . ."

"Sure, but first we should move because they are intending to catch us so bad." And she points at tiny flying things coming out of a huge covered object.

"What in the hell is this? Are they the Plonsters?"

"We have to move quickly," Jollya replies.

I feel so dizzy with such a headache, and my face is hurting, but I'm trying to hold on and just keep moving with Jollya.

"Here! We need to open the sewer cover, hurry up honey," she says when we stop among the ruined buildings. I start lifting the heavy cover with Jollya.

"After you, babe," I say, nodding to the open nasty gap.

After she jumps inside, I get in slowly using the ladder, and I use all my power to pull the cover back and close it.

"Come on, honey; get down and move on!" she says, but at this moment I feel really sick and dizzy, so I just let my body land on the dirty, watery floor.

*

I wake up in a barely lit room that has a feeling of wetness, and Jollya is sitting beside me.

"Harley, do you feel any better now?"

"I fell on the ground and . . . I don't remember what happened next . . ."

"You were tired and in need of sleep; you slept about ten hours."

"I'm starving also. Where are we?"

"Dallecus, a city under the ground . . ."

I nod and sigh to recover my mind and my memory, but nothing comes to my mind except Nopoly, the perfect city, and the last peaceful moments I had there.

"I shouldn't disobey the order and what they asked me to do . . . I saw them in my dream killing the child for real!" I say while I'm crying because I feel kind of down over the consequences of disobeying the orders and escaping from the city.

"You should, and you did. You'll never kill a human being in cold blood . . ."

"They said that my bullets were blank; they only wanted to see if I'm—"

"The issue is bigger than you imagine . . ." she interrupts me.

"Where are all the demons?" I look around, terrified.

"They're inside every single one of us. But Nopoly, where they're manipulating humans, is a place of pure evil . . ."

"I was there. None of what you are saying is making any sense! Unless I was in another world and . . . and another life before you came and took that creepy mask off my face, taking me to this new universe. What was that mask? I was in such a rush that I forgot to ask you about it. I . . . I can't identify which life I'm living now . . ."

She looks at the mask that she holds, saying:

"You were under the VI effect . . ."

"VI! What is that?"

"It's a Virtual Illusion mask which allows you to see things totally differently according to the one who set this up: the guider . . ."

I get confused because I didn't understand a word, and I express that confusion with the irregular movements of my head; I can't form any words to ask Jollya the hundred questions I have. She puts that weird mask, that has thin wires, in front of my face saying:

"This is the VI mask that you had on your face like all the other citizens of Nopoly, and with this, you were able to see me as a demon . . . a demon that wanted to take off your face with a scary look . . ."

"But they told us in Nopoly that we are the only survivors of the humans who are left in this universe . . . Wait a minute! What did you say about seeing you as a demon?!"

"With this mask, the guider could control your brain; your brain was being tricked when you were watching through this thing. You couldn't identify the objects you saw in their real pictures, and that was the trick to this technology. See, it's similar to the VR that we all know, but this VI can turn the reality into an illusion inside your head by changing what you see relative to the data that has been uploaded from the guider's perspective there. And when the sight is controlled, the whole behavior will be too."

I'm considering the idea, which could be real but insane at the same time. Jollya draws my attention again by taking a pen from the dusty table and pointing the pen at me.

"Let's say this is a pen in reality, and someone has added to its data that any pen you will see through this mask is a knife; so, basically, when you have the VI mask on your face and you see me with the knife instead of seeing the pen in my hand, what are you going to do?" I drop my head, replying:

"I'll try to defend myself . . ."

"Exactly, and it is all my fault that I have just a pen to draw a heart on your hand."

I don't feel the pen's prick as I do with my heartbeats . . .

"Do you mean that all the demons weren't demons?!" I say with a low, broken voice.

She does what I was afraid of by nodding yes with falling tears. I stand up directly with wide open eyes, putting my hands on my head and feeling that I'm about to go crazy.

"I can't believe it, how is that possible?! That's insane!" I scream at the pain and guilt I feel.

Jollya puts her head down, hugging me and wetting me with her warm tears. But then, I remember when I refused to kill, when I realized that my target was a human being.

“Listen, this isn’t the worst part of the story . . .” Jollya adds before we hear a knock on the door.

“Come in if it’s Patema,” Jollya shouts and the door opens.

“Yes, it’s me with the food,” a lady with a cover on her head and a wide smile says. “And I know that you guys are hungry for sure. Dig in!” she continues, putting two plates on the old-fashioned table. The food looks like grass with chicken on it.

“Thank you, sister, your food is always amazing just like you,” Jollya says, smiling.

“No problem habibti, this dish is called Molokhia with chicken; it was the favorite dish of my son Ali,” she says before she leaves with a tear on her cheek.

Just before I open my mouth, Jollya starts to talk, trying to hide her sorrow:

“Her son has been taken for a while and she can’t stop thinking about him. I’m amazed at how powerful this woman is. She is one of the cooks who are feeding people who live here. Even though she is missing Ali, she is working for the community. There is no option of giving up, honey.”

“If she is a good mom, she has to search for her son and find him at any cost, right? And this Moloko tastes so good!” I say this with a mouthful of that food.

“She believes in the unity of society and destiny, and she always says that we are like one body; when any part of the body gets hurt, the whole body will feel the pain. And it’s called Molokhia . . .”

"Now this is ridiculous. How do we have the same destiny? We are different and that means we have a different destiny!"

"The same destiny comes because we have the same enemy . . ."

"And what is our destiny and who is the enemy?"

"Our destiny is to fight the evil until we end it or die trying."

I hit the spoon on the table, saying:

"You have been infected with that Patema's thoughts. Your mind has become a terrorist mind!" I take Jollya by her shoulder, whispering into her ear:

"Listen! I'll never fight nor die for nobody!"

Jollya holds my arms gently, saying:

"You will because I'll—" I take her hand, interrupting:

"What is the purpose of doing that in such a new universe like this?"

"We have to go out and look for the little Ali, and on our way, I'll let you know some of the thing you really want to know, as I promised." I sigh a long sigh, asking:

"How old is he?"

"Around eight years . . ."

I nod sadly, saying:

"How did that Patema lose her son?"

"It took you a while to ask this question . . ."

“Because, honestly, I don’t care about her or her son. All I care about is you, Jollya.”

She looks at the empty plate, saying:

“Ali was taken by kidnappers called the Explorers Army who work for the Nopoly government.”

“Hold on, hold on! WHAT?! Are you out of your mind? This army I was about to . . . be with . . .” I calm myself, continuing, “it’s an army for bringing the energy and the food from outside the city.”

“Yeah, that’s what they taught you!”

“No! This Patema must be lying, don’t trust her anymore!”

“You may have forgotten what Feller Rock called you at the beginning of the Explorers test—”

“A kidnapper . . . But how did you know that?” I interrupt, remembering everything that happened in the Hidden Arena . . .

“I told you that I’m going to tell you everything at the right time. Now take this gas mask and follow me because I want to show you something very important outside.”

I look at the reflection the glass makes, and I see tired eyes that want to rest for at least a week, but anyway, let’s see what she wants to show me.

10- Poor Ones

We're walking among the people who are living in Dallecus which is just a huge, wet, and dirty shelter; it's reminds me of the games I used to play when I was a kid.

A band of men comes up to us, one of whom says:

"Are we moving now Jollya?"

"Not now Sami, but soon," Jollya responds.

Most of the people here look miserably unhappy, looking at me with their dry and tired eyes; I hate to be part of a weak group. The test of power I underwent in Nopoly may have ruined my empathy . . . I don't know, but I don't like this atmosphere at all.

"Harley, be ready! We are going to go out to the hell again, so put the mask on," Jollya says when we approach the exit room of the city.

After climbing the ladder, I open the sewer cover.

"Carefully! And see if anyone is around or anything in the sky." I do what she asks and we both get out safely, but the place here outside doesn't seem safe, not a bit! A black rain is falling, leaving dark spots on the burnt ground.

"What a place! I bet it's worse than our ruined world."

"Harley, there is no fifth universe, there is no seventh, nor a multi-universe. It's the same world, our world and the same universe. The multi-universe is just a theory which has been used in Nopoly to persuade you of the new style of the city, to stop you from asking about the city or to talk about yourselves. Everyone in the city, they think they came from the seventh universe, exactly like you were thinking there, and everyone is afraid to talk about that, including you when you were in there. Even the dimensional tears were totally fake; the glasses you put before we started our journey were nothing but VR glasses . . ."

My brain can't take it, why do they need to do that? But I decide to ask this question instead:

"How did you know about all of that?"

"Well, because I was in the city and I've collected so much information about Nopoly."

"And again, how?"

"By taking a couple of Nopolyens' faces . . . Why do you think some people get disappeared?"

I stop and cross my arms, saying skeptically:

"That was impossible and so dangerous! How could you do that?!"

"Thanks to my sleeping needles . . ." she says, smiling.

"Right, the same needle you used on me in your first attempt to get me out of the city. But, what about the cameras in the city? And what did you do to the people you took the masks from?"

"It was a diluted dose that I used on you just to calm you down; and it wasn't that hard to cut off the cameras for a while, and when the flying cameras came to me to check what was wrong, I told the people who are watching through these cameras that maybe something was wrong with the cameras after hiding the original face carrier that I borrowed."

I'm so astonished at the process Jollya used and her bravery.

"Damn, that was so smart. But did you do all of that just to get some information?"

"A lot of information. When I was carrying the face, I lived their lives, read their books, and saw their memories."

"As I did by seeing John Cooper's memory!"

"Exactly, but those memories were fake, and the data came directly into your brain to persuade you to do things or believe other things."

"Didn't you get affected by believing in these data when you had the mask on?" I ask Jollya, stepping on dead bodies.

"Careful!" she replies, pointing to them to avoid us trampling them. "Another poor family . . . Back to our subject; no, I wasn't affected because I knew that was all fake," she continues.

I start to consider her claim and what I've been through, and I become so skeptical about everything.

"How can I trust that what you are saying is the truth? What makes all of this real?!" Jollya stops walking and looks at me with crossed arms, saying:

"Did you forget who I am, Harley?!"

"Maybe you're not the real one, maybe all of this is a dream or some kind of simulation. What is the evidence that makes all of these crazy things you talked about make sense?"

"There are many pieces of evidence, but first, you need to trust your wife who saved your life; what about that?"

"Okay, okay. So, based on what you've said, we are living in the world that had been destroyed because of the damn triangle communist and Shi'ite countries, which I hate—"

"Harley, Harley! First of all, we don't need to hate anyone; second, let's agree that every single idea or piece of information you got from Nopoly is totally false, okay?" she says before she gets down, telling me to do the same because the Plonsters in the red sky are getting closer and it seems that they have been looking for us all this time.

After a while, the sky gets clearer, although it is not really clear of the black smoke and red color that cover it, hiding the sunlight.

"You said that all the information that I have from Nopoly is false, so you'll need to tell me the real reason for this mess!" I demand, pointing at the ashy air.

"No, I'm going to make the responsible for all of this tell you soon—"

"Do you know who is responsible? I'm going to murder him! I'm telling you . . ." I interrupt, but she starts laughing, saying:

"You'll like him . . ."

"Excuse me?! Have you lost your mind because of the radiation in the area?"

"Haha, NO!"

I don't understand Jollya right now, and I have so many points that need to be explained, but I have to calm down to see what Jollya wants to show me, and I really want to meet the guy who is responsible for this situation to hear from him just what happened, and then he'll meet his destiny; I'm going to exact our nation's revenge on him.

"From now on I'm your commander and you'll have to obey me. No action without my orders; is it clear soldier?" Jollya says sweetly in an attempt at being the boss here.

"Haha, now I miss the old commander in Nopoly," I reply.

"Shhh! Just follow me."

"Okay, okay . . ."

We continue walking and jumping over the rubble till Jollya stops behind a ruined wall, crouching and saying:

"Plonsters! Let's hide here for a while."

"Beware of the fire!"

"Don't worry; our suits can stand the heat of the sun, but I can't promise that yours will protect you from me."

After about a half hour of walking, I start seeing the huge barrier of Nopoly.

"Crouch and come closer," Jollya says carefully.

"Do you want to burn me?"

"Seriously, come and watch; they are far away, but you can see them . . ." She points to the band of soldiers.

"Whom do they belong to?"

"These are the Explorers Army. Look what was waiting for you if you would've passed the test and were one of them . . ."

I barely see them going around with their weapons, and then they disappear inside a renovated but half-destroyed building that is supported by some pieces of shed tin, so I start to move to see clearly, but Jollya's hand stops me and she says:

"Patience! They'll appear again."

I'm waiting and calming myself while I'm burning from inside to know what they are doing there. After about ten minutes, we hear a rain of gunshots from afar. The soldiers appear, dragging three children with them.

"What are they doing? Don't tell me what I see is real!" and I shake my head in case I'm hallucinating.

"It's real, Harley," Jollya responds sadly.

"WAIT! You scum! What are you d—"

"Shhhhh! Don't be dumb. They'll kill both of us if they see we are watching them!" Jollya almost climbs on me to calm me down.

"They've taken the kids with them! Why? . . . Where?"

"Wait till they drive away. I promised you that you're going to know everything."

They are gone with the poor kids, and they are driving toward Nopoly! I really wanted to save them, but they've disappeared now, so we move to the place that the kids were taken from. We come to the spot where the soldiers were, and what a view!

"Oh God, I told them; this place isn't safe for anyone here at all." Jollya checks if anyone is still alive. "I promise you that we'll save all your kids, I promise . . ." she continues, crying, before she turns to the other room of the building, leaving the dead bodies lying on the ground and drowning in their blood. The view is so scary and inhumane. I feel so sick and cold that

I can't stand on my feet, so I fall to my knees on the bloody floor with blurry vision; but Jollya's voice wakes my brain up.

"Oh my God!" I jump up after hearing that and run to her so fast to see what is going on. I see Jollya with a child, a little beautiful child hiding under a huge black metal sheet and covering her face with some kind of white fabric that is mixed with a touch of black.

"I can't believe it, you're alive!" Jollya takes the child, hugging her with tears running down. "She's so lucky to be hiding under lead, which prevents them seeing her by infrared."

I feel better to see this child alive, even though she doesn't look like an American to me . . .

While Jollya is trying to explain to her that she'll have to come with us because it's cold here, I open my bag to pick up a gas mask for her little face, but the child starts crying out for her mom. I come to the child, who looks about four years old, looking into her sad eyes and telling her that her mom is waiting for her in our place and everything will be okay.

"But Dad said: 'Don't go with strangers!'" the little child whimpers.

"You are in a very cold place, little angel, and your mom told us to bring you to a better place," Jollya responds.

"Is she there?"

"She is in a better place . . ." Jollya says, helping the girl put the gas mask on properly with the little suit.

I don't know why Jollya has lied to this little girl, but I really don't want the girl to see her mom covered with blood among the dead bodies. I cover all the bodies with sheets so that the child doesn't see them in this hideous state, but the blood is running everywhere.

"Here we go. Everything will be okay, don't worry," I say to the girl, but surprisingly, Jollya picks up the child, who seems calm and comfortable and falls asleep.

"You have your magic!" I look at Jollya, smiling.

"We have to get back quickly before she wakes up!" Jolly whispers to me.

That was an amazing surprise that my crazy Jollya got this girl to sleep, but it's the best way to get her out of here without getting a shock she'll never forget in her entire life.

*

We continue walking for an hour, and before we get closer to the place underground, I remember the reason we are out.

"Jollya! What about Ali?! We went out to find him, right?"

"Now, you know who is responsible for his disappearance and where he is with all the other kids, right?"

"Other kids? What do you mean?"

"Shhh! Don't wake her, baby. We'll talk about it later."

Jollya has no clue what is happening inside me. Every minute that passes, my questions increase and my curiosity grows, but I have to be patient.

The weather is getting so windy and dusty that we can barely see our hands. We are walking to nowhere, hoping we don't end up in a hole or over some cliff, so I use a green flashlight.

A couple minutes later and another green light starts to flash from afar.

"This is the signal! Harley, follow the light honey!"

"Yes sir!"

Jollya is carrying the child, and I carry my bag and hers, so it's hard to move with the heavy storm, but after a long struggle, we succeed in arriving at the guy, who is holding the green light and waving with it.

"That was so hard to find our way with this weather, thanks Josef," Jollya says to the guy.

"No problem. Now get in, hurry up!" he says, and we get inside and finally get some peace and quiet after that crazy weather, but after getting underground, we feel like the ground is moving; it's like an earthquake!

"You woke up, our little angel!" Jollya says in a shaky voice.

The girl looks so confused and scared, so I try to hold Jollya and the child still by hugging them while holding onto a pipe on the wall with my all might to keep steady.

"Thank you honey, but that's something normal . . ." Jollya says.

"To have crazy weather and earthquakes?!" And she nods yes.

We get inside, and the little girl is still looking around so confused, calling for her mom. I put my hand on the girl's head, telling her:

"Don't worry, little girl. What's your name?" I ask her, but she refuses to tell me, hiding her face with Jollya's shoulder. Jollya signals to me to let her be and touches the girl's back to calm her.

Jollya enters a room with the girl and two ladies, who seem so sweet and nice, and I wait outside, watching Dallecus and hearing poor people's voices sing with their different dialects and basic instruments. They're so poor after what happened to them, especially the parents who lost their children to those kidnappers. I can't imagine that my previous goal, the Explorers Army, has become my enemy now. Freaking villainous . . .

Jollya comes out and heads to me with a cheerful face, thanking and hugging me without any mention of the reason.

"This is you without any stupid ideas or hate speech: a nice, helpful man, full of humanity."

"Thank you Jollya. I was socialized and affected by the Bezman methodology that was controlling me somehow . . ."

Jollya proposes to rest after the awful journey we had, and I agree with this heavenly proposition.

11- Going Back in Time

"Jollya!" I wake up, missing my wife in the bed, before I find her reading a book.

"You scared me! Haha . . ." Jollya responds with a hand on her heart. "How was your sleep?"

"Sorry, but I had a terrifying nightmare . . ."

"What was it?"

"It was bloody scary. I remember that I was drowning in dead bodies and limbs; I got myself out after a great struggle, drenched in blood, and I started running away from the place, but I ended up somewhere else, which was slightly filled with blood, with many ruined small dolls floating on the surface. And then, a little girl was running toward me crying and . . . and she seemed scared. And she stopped about a meter away from me; I tried to talk to her, but she didn't answer, so I came to her slowly, but she looked at me with black bloody eyes holding my hands and screaming before she burst into flames. I pulled my hands away from her while she was burning, and the flames grew higher before they faded away, showing me a young lady; she was crying in silence, looking at me so sadly, before she turned and glitchily faded away."

I cover my face with my hands, trying to clear these scenes from my memory, but I can't forget this creepy dream. Jollya comes to me, telling me it was just a dream.

"I think we should've adopted that little girl; maybe this dream is a sign to take care of her. You know, I've always wished we had a beautiful girl, just like you. I'd call her . . . Lori, my beautiful Jollyn," I say, winking at her and smiling.

But Jollya looks at the ground with a little smile that clashes with the tears she sheds.

I get confused because I thought it was a nice joke, but the silence hangs in the room. While I'm drying her warm tears, she holds my hand, kissing it, and I do the same thing with her beautiful hand, telling her:

"These tears mean that you're missing someone. Tell me; who do you miss except me? Your parents?" I ask her and she shakes her head.

"Then who?!"

"I absolutely miss them, but . . ."

"But what?!" I ask hastily.

"Promise me that you'll not get angry nor do any impulsive action!"

"What is it Jollya? Tell me please!"

"Promise!"

"I do! Tell me now!"

"We are going to meet the people who are responsible for all this . . ."

"I thought it was only one guy!"

"That's right, the idea comes from one guy, but the implementers are a group of people . . ."

"I'll be patient till I hear everything from them."

"You'll not just hear, but you'll see also . . ."

"See?!" And Jollya nods yes.

She starts to move out of this wet room, and I follow her. We get inside an old elevator before another stranger who has thick black hair gets in.

"Are you coming with us?" I ask him, and he responds coldly: "Yes, I am."

While we are going down, I look at Jollya telling her that I'm uncomfortable, and she starts, saying:

"Honey, this is Tabi. He is one of the Free Ones who saved me from dying."

"Dying? When?! And how?!"

"How many times have I told you that you'll know everything soon, my curious love," Jollya says, giving me an innocent sweet smile, so I don't have anything to say except to nod okay, especially since I've got a headache with an annoying tinnitus.

"We are getting close to Camelos, so be prepared," says this Tabi with a clipped tone.

When we arrive at the meeting room, the door is open, but surprisingly there is no one in the room, which is full of pictures of children.

"What a creepy disgusting person! What is he doing with all these children's pictures?!" I say while looking at a little girl who draws my attention; I look at the girl again with a little more focus, and I feel the rush in my heart and the pain in my stomach. I've seen this girl before, but what is killing me is that I can't identify who she is. At that moment I feel a hand on my shoulder that wakes my brain up; it's Jollya's hand. And then, a sound comes from above saying:

"Welcome Mr. and Mrs. Woodman. I'm Camelos. Please have a seat and relax before we start our journey into the past—"

"What do you mean by that?!"

"Don't interrupt me, please! To find answers to your unlimited questions, Mr. Harley, you have to trust me as your wife does."

"What is he talking about? Jollya, do you truly trust this guy?!"

"Honey, you trust me, right? And I do trust this man because he helped me find you, and—"

"You told me that he was responsible for all of this mess," I try to whisper but sound irritated.

"Mr. Harley! Do you want to go back in time to recover your memory?!" the man says confidently.

"Yes, I do!" I shout before two pairs of glasses with headphones slide down the table that we are supposed to sit at. I look at Jollya quizzically, asking:

"Seriously! Another VI experience?" And I turn to the screens continuing, "Are you joking?! I won't put this crap on my face again."

"It's VRM glasses. There is a huge difference between the VI and the VRM, even in the pronunciation, isn't there?" Jollya says, smiling faintly.

"Virtual Reality for Memories is a technology that can show you what another person saw in the past. For example, Jollya will let you see what she lived through in a certain time of her life by translating her memories to a vision you can see, and this operation will happen by a connection with her head.

The difference between these glasses and the VI ones is that you'll be able to control your brain and use it to analyze what you'll see. In addition, what you'll see via the VRM is just pictures in Jollya's memory that can't harm either you or her in any way," Camelos clarifies.

"It sounds so crazy. I might react to what I see; wouldn't that be dangerous?"

"Don't worry baby. As he said, this is a totally different technology, and you can take off the VRM any time you want. Unlike the VI, which controlled your sight, using VRM will not get anyone hurt or killed because you'll have free will the whole time," Jollya says.

"Please don't remind me . . . I guess I get it," I say softly, and when I see Jollya is waiting for me and holding the glasses in her hands with a little smile on her face, I take the glasses to look at them closely.

Now, the VRM glasses are covering my eyes, blinding me from seeing anything but the darkness.

"Perfect! Now, are you ready guys?" that crazy man says through the microphone.

"Only for you Jollya . . ." I utter.

The first thing I see is a glitchy image that is confusing me with its various colors.

"There's something wrong with this crap!" I can't hear any reply, and just before I take off this thing on my face, I see an open door in the distance and someone is waiting for my entrance, so my curiosity draws me nearer. I start walking, jogging, and running to find that door and the person who starts to become clear to my vision. It's a guy I've never seen before who has cold green eyes and no facial expression. He signals me to come through the door, and I obey to see what is going to happen next, but another glitch hits my vision and the guy has disappeared.

I look around to see where he went and where I am, but I realize that the door has become a mirror that reflects that guy's cold face.

"Where am I? Where did you go, man?" I say without hearing my own voice! It's so terrifying because it feels like I've become deaf.

"Now, you are in my position in the past, Harley; you'll see my memories, watching what I saw and hearing what I heard. We can hear you, but you aren't able to hear anything outside my memories, so you are my eyes in the past now. Your wife will be under these conditions too, and don't worry; you can end this by taking off the VRM if you want," Camelos responds, which takes away the thought of being deaf.

I raise both my hands to touch the glasses, and it feels like I'm the one who is controlling myself, so that's good so far.

The view starts with a glitchy image, and Camelos, who I'm seeing through his eyes, takes the phone from his pocket. He rings someone called Wildduck1, saying:

"Ready for tomorrow's celebration?"

"Yes Dr.1, love you."

"Thanks. don't forget at twelve in your time, we'll all come. Love you, bye." Camelos ends the call and then scrolls through names. All the numbers have weird names: India1, Mine1, New1, Orange1, Very1, and so many others.

A quick flash of light takes me to a moment when this guy is standing and telling someone beside him, who looks like a young lady, that he'll throw the biggest party ever today, and then they both jump in a car. The area they are driving in looks so awful because of the homeless who are lying everywhere, the trash, and the slums. And because there is at least one police car at every corner, with police-drones flying everywhere too. In fact, a police officer is stopping us.

"Hello officer," Camelos says.

"I.DD detected!" a robot officer utters before it scans my—I mean, Camelos's—head and the lady's.

"Where—"

"The Delbury Center," Camelos answers, interrupting.

"Why?"

"Celebration, hahaha."

"What's in the baggage?"

"Go and check the fireworks, they'll decorate the sky."

"Have fun!" it says after scanning everything in the car.

While he is driving, a flashlight appears from afar and gets close till it blinds me for a while. When the light fades away, I see clearly that we have stopped to get out of the car; Camelos takes two boxes of fireworks from the baggage, saying:

"Let's celebrate, my friend!" After the security scan and the check, we go into an enormous arena that contains a huge number of people, cybers, and robots; and everyone looks beautiful and super modern with their lights, neon, and UV tattoos. But I'm wondering what this gathering is, and the answer comes with little kids singing:

"Everyone across the corner is coming here

Yaaah

We'll sing and dance to make this year

Yaaah

Happy New Year, Happy New Year

Happy New Year, Hurrah!"

"It's our turn to make this year kid . . ." Camelos says to one of these kids who are singing around me while I—he—picks up hundreds of the fireworks and starts handing them out to the kids. More and more kids and adults are getting bundles of these little rockets with smiles on their faces. After this sharing, the lady who was with Camelos in the car opens the last box, preparing the rest of the fireworks for launch.

"Are you ready guys?!" Camelos is shouting.

"Easy! My ear!" I say, but obviously without hearing myself.

A little guy who didn't accept the fireworks from Camelos is looking at me doubtfully.

"This kid looks uncomfortable to see you Camelos . . ."

"I was almost flying with happiness in that moment, my friend," Camelos replies.

"You mean you were high; and I'm not your friend!" I say, trying to abuse him.

"Being high on drugs wasn't bad at that time, but I wasn't anyway. That kid didn't know that I was levitating with happiness and the satisfaction of a successful start to our plan . . ."

“What plan?” I question him.

“The Small Changers.”

“What the hell is that?”

“To change huge things, you need small ones’ help, as I did by giving these little kids the way to change the whole United States of America.”

“What do you mean?!”

“Three years it took for us to produce the Super-Nano Ants, of which millions are inside the rockets of the fireworks. And with the help of a thousand Free Ones across this country and some assistance from these little pure hands,” he says, pointing at the kids, “the Super-Nano Ants will be spread across the sky of our strong, modern, and unfair country.”

“Are you done talking? What the hell are you talking about?! Explain one thing you have just chattered about!” I feel that I’m shouting because my veins start throbbing.

“I’ll explain the whole process, but first, I’ll show you the reasons for the Small Changers plan by showing you how life was under the Big-Data system first.” He takes me to a small cramped room full of running screens and a dirty table covered in papers and tools; it seems we are in a hidden place like a garage or shelter. The first thing I see on the screen is a video of a little black kid getting shot in his tummy. I am shocked by what I see.

“Why?! What did he do to deserve this!”

“‘*By mistake*,’ the police *said*. And the thing is, the police didn’t tell the truth until two guys showed the whole world what really happened to the kid by filming the accident. The police said before this video was revealed that someone from the next church killed that kid for peeing beside the church. But what happened is the police went to catch someone in the hood, and the officer missed the shot; that's according to the police."

"That can't be!" I respond, but because I can't hear myself, I remove the VRM with a rising heartbeat. "You're a liar. That would never happen. You made all this up to justify what you did . . ."

"I don't need to justify anything to you! I can simply end your life . . ."

Jollya looks at me saying hastily:

"But that's not what Camelos wants, and—"

"So, you're pretty much on his side! Wow!" I interrupt Jollya.

"No! I want you to recover your memory; you don't need to be convinced, just watch and remember our life before the nuclear war."

Wait! she's right; I start to remember that it was poor people living on the outskirts of the cities, and they had a hard life there.

I take a long breath before I put the VRM on my face again and sit and wait for what's next.

"Before moving on, let me just tell you that it wasn't one incident, but over a thousand kids got killed in the same way with different stories from the police!"

I'm depressed about what he said, especially with all the pictures and videos that I see about these cases.

"I can take no more. Stop showing me that!" I say while closing my eyes to avoid seeing another tragedy.

It ends with a bright flash that takes me in turn to a place that looks like a popular neighborhood, which is a little bit darker and so much dirtier than the place we were in. The people who live in this place are so scary; black spots are all around their eyes, and their clothes are totally torn. Screams and shouts come from every corner with one light in each street; this makes the atmosphere dreadful and uncomfortable to see.

"What is this place? Why do you bring us here?"

"Harley, this is my home where I spent my childhood—"

"Who cares?! It's not my business where the hell you were raised. I'll take off the damn VRM if you want me to see more of these . . . nasty things."

"Unfortunately, you can't remove it now because this'll explain a lot for you. Keep in mind that over twenty million Americans lived in this kind of environment; all because they didn't fit with modern society by rejecting the New Generation Plan."

"And what the hell was that?"

"Let me first put the Identity Data—or what I call a barcode—on my temple." And he stands in front of the mirror, taking a piece of thin black chip to paste on his head, sticking it on with some kind of tool. Slowly I remember something about this IDD, and I remember I used to have one on my head. That chip—.

"Look! With this chip, police-drones can identify who you are, and they can take a look at the information in your Civil Profile while you're walking down the street. Now guess how many people have been killed by mistake just because someone has hacked those flying things . . . And I know many poor people have been accused of hacking cases and getting punished without even reliable evidence," Camelos says, interrupting my thoughts.

I do remember something like this happened; a lot of cases have happened actually, but I can't say that because it'd be such a shame to admit that.

"And that is assuming that these cameras have been hacked for real. Anyway, the problem with this chip is it has to be tattooed on the skin, and to fake it like I do, the IDD location needs to be branded by fire and complex operations of hacking to be in the Big-Data system," he continues.

"I don't think the government accused you for no reason. Here you are; you admitted that you hacked the system to be registered in . . . Dastro," I respond, amazed by the fact I remember the name of the Big-Data program.

"We're doing pretty good with the recovery of your memory. Harley, I hacked the system at the age of twenty-one; I grew up in an atmosphere where I was told that I didn't deserve to live, and neither did my parents and a hundred million Americans in the USA because we thought that freedom included freedom of belief, but we were wrong.

"People who refused that IDD tattoo weren't in the Dastro program, and because of that they had no free health care, very poor chances of finding work, no right to get a loan from the banks, and no free education for their kids, who could have the IDD when they turned twelve because at that age the kids had the right to decide for themselves without the parents' say-so. Have a look at some of the political decisions," Camelos says, showing me messages between the politicians saying that they are looking for a generation dependent only on technology; a generation that can be controlled by these particular politicians.

"All they want is to have more control, which leads to more power, and that leads in its turn to more money; and it is easy to control the small minds, isn't it, Harley?"

"Because with the money you can have anything you want!"

"Talking about the money; to reduce the population, the media supports all kinds of acts that can lessen the birth rate for certain politicians' benefit. To refresh your memory, I'll remind you of the Love Demonstration, and the banners that they all have from the movie *Humophobe* that encouraged people to marry who the hell they want, including robots or as the media called them, Humo. The genetic editing was so easy to use by the kids; not to mention that it had been officially used in the American military many years before. At twelve years old kids could make huge changes to their bodies by their own will; and becoming genetically edited was something encouraged by the society, also thanks to the media. Not to mention the illegal methods that changed the look and shape of humans, regardless of their age," he utters, taking me to a place full of young people and robots who are shouting and repeating:

"The Love . . . All We Need to Have!"

And then I'm taken to another demonstration where the people are saying:

"The Love Has No Matter, No Gender, No Guider!"

I remember these kinds of demonstrators, and it feels like I'm with them, and supporting the idea of love is the most important thing to live with. I didn't have any problem with these banners at all. It's so amazing to see all these people have one goal, love, only love. And there are not only humans in this demonstration but also the cybers and the robots.

“Thanks for bringing me back to my old perfect life . . .”

“It wasn’t perfect for groups of people and—”

“*I don’t care!*” I respond, interrupting him.

“Eh . . . it wasn’t quite perfect for you either as a big shooting trainer in the police. And don’t interrupt me, please!”

“My patience is running out because of blaming everything on the government, and now you start talking about us as a . . .”

“The Chosen Class! Keep in mind that it was not the whole government that had a lack of humanity, but some of the politicians in it, who wanted to get rid of the people who couldn’t accept this situation, who didn’t want to be just a number in the society which could be removed at any time, who didn’t want to lose their children in the name of fake love, and the people who didn’t want to lose their identity and forget their history; those people were the minority or Outferios Class.

“Away from politics, even the society put pressure on the Outferios; it was recommended and sometimes required to have cyberware, which can help in having a better chance of getting a job with these powerful modern cyber limbs.”

I have a cyber forearm sins I was twenty-one, and I’ve always thought that it’s so cool to have cyber part, and it can be useful in many ways. But why couldn’t I realize my cyber arm in Nopoly?!

“The people who didn’t accept being in society, didn’t need to live in it; it’s that simple. People have the freedom to live the way they like; and having cyberware wasn’t an order from the government, but the people liked having pieces of art in their bodies, that's it," I respond, speaking proudly for living in the Chosen Class.

"Harley, you were just like the others; socialized! The men liked to be cyber to look more attractive and stronger (thanks to the movies that always showed the heroes with these kinds of iron parts in their bodies). On the other side, women, from the beginning of civilization, were searching for immortal beauty and they like to show it by following modern fashion. So, imagine a perfectly shaped part of your body that can be colored and designed in the way you like, how cool is that?"

"It was so cool seeing that on people. My arm is optimized as well; so, in the end, the people had the free choice."

"You've missed a lot . . . Let me show you the hidden reasons for all this media propaganda . . ." Camelos says, taking me again to his tiny garage. He starts showing me the decisions that came from some politicians; they supported the Chosen Class and seizing the people who didn't fit in the New Generation Plan, which would help the Big-Data system to be stronger and more acceptable to Americans.

"The plan is to invest in the Chosen Class by controlling them and taking advantage of them. Examples of that: buying tobacco, drugs, digital drugs, and the cyber parts. Look at the information we have about the cyber parts; it makes the organ trade legal for the limb-doctors. The parts that have been cut out are worth millions of dollars in India for example," Camelos says while he's showing me some evidence of buying the human organs.

"The government had nothing to do with all of these abuses because the private companies were taking control of all the business in America . . ." I respond.

"Right, but the big bosses of all companies were related to people in the government who were looking for an empty-minded nation; so, those who didn't want to have any sort of tattoo on their bodies, just a barcode on the temple, who didn't want to dissolve into a materialistic worldview that adopted fake freedom, and who were against the Big-Data system in general because of human rights matters, were isolated in all different ways—"

"Human rights? What is this excuse you throw now?!" I interrupt Camelos.

"Scientific experiments on humans were the most terrifying thing, which the Outferios totally opposed," he says, showing me horrible pictures of monsters were humans. I do remember; all the experiments were either to find a new breed of being to support the evolution theory, or to have stronger, smarter, immortal humans; all the experiments had terrible consequences (thanks to the damn professional hackers that revealed these secrets and more . . .)

"By the time, all these actions forced millions and millions to move out of the Chosen Class' cities. This is our past . . ." Camelos ends his speech with a sad broken voice while taking me back to the top of a building, showing me Delaware.

"I believed that everything the government was doing was an attempt to make our life better . . . or even perfect."

"Just to remind you, the people who refused to be under that perfect system, and refused to move outside the city, somewhere away from the Chosen Class's places, were the small minorities in the Chosen Class or as they've been called Inferios, as we needed more of a split in the society so we had this designation," Camelos says emotionally.

"Yeah, I remember that the cleaner of my office was Inferios; and nothing went wrong and everything was perfect! So, what's your point?"

"This system was perfect for the Chosen Class, those who wanted to make money and live a life ignoring morality and others' lives. None of the Outferios nor Inferios was in a high position in society; none of them were able to change a thing in the land of freedom—"

"The civilization had to continue whether with your people or not. We had the law and the system; and the government saw, that with this system, we could be protected from the terrorism, huge crimes, etc . . ." I say while looking at my civilized city.

"You . . . you are brainwashed. Just think about it and be objective. Is it believable that no one from 'my people,' as you said, had no intelligence to reach the top in this land? And the best way to be protected from terrorism was the societies-isolation and societies-election? Where was the terrorism? Was it inside every single one of the hundred million American who were the Inferios in the eyes of Dastro's slaves, as the Nopoly government consider me and you now?"

"I'm getting sick and tired of your speech. What really makes me continue this journey is seeing my beautiful city which helps me memorize my perfect past . . . Now, I'll leave the rest of your sad story for you . . ." I say, taking off the VRM because now I've had enough of this hate speech. That was our life; I know that it wasn't perfect for everyone, but I was happy and this was the life.

"But you don't know the whole story yet . . ." Camelos says, but I pay him no attention. I'm done with this drama.

12- The Small Changers

“Jollya, I’m out of here; are you coming?” I say to Jollya who is looking at the VRM sadly. Just before I reach Jollya, the room starts sinking into darkness so I can’t see anything around me.

“Okay now, can you turn the lights up because I’m done with this?” But silence hangs over the place and I get no response.

“WHAT NOW?!” I shout, but it is still quiet and there’s no answer, so I decide to walk carefully toward Jollya. I walk and continue walking, and it feels like I’m walking in a circle!

After a period of screaming and blind running, I stop, looking at the low lighting that comes from the VRM; I’m thinking about putting them on again to see the end of this stupid story.

The first thing I see after putting the VRM on is a little child in the distance with another grown man, and Jollya stands nearer to me with closed eyes and a sad face. I start running toward Jollya but she just fades away, and I remember that I’m in the virtual world that has been created by someone’s memory. Am I connected with Jollya now?

I continue walking to the child and the man who is holding her hand, to figure out who they are, but when I get closer to them, the little child has faded away also!

The man is standing still, and surprisingly the man is Camelos! I’ll do what I’ve really wanted to do for a while; I raise my fist, and once I touch his cold face, I again go inside his stupid memory to see through his eyes. He’s standing among a huge number of citizens, and the kids are singing and celebrating with their sparkle sticks and lasers.

"Happy New Year My Beautiful World!" Camelos shouts before launching the fireworks.

"Bang, Bang . . . Bang, Bang . . ." the fireworks are lighting up the dark sky, turning the atmosphere into a bright and colorful night.

A couple minutes later, and the hustle and bustle from the crowd turns into silence, which hangs over the place for a full minute; but after that creepy unexpected silence, the chaos starts taking control; everyone looks at their mobiles; some of them look dreadful, and the rest are turning crazy. Camelos starts running insanely fast with his friend who was with him in the car.

"What is happening, are you crazy?!" I scream while I'm hearing the police sirens all over the city.

"Camelos! What have you done? Why has everyone turned to this state?!"

"I did nothing but shut down the electricity and the internet all over America . . ."

"What?!"

I'm immobilized right now while this mad guy is running and getting underground with his assistant.

"Dr.2, hurry up!" Camelos shouts before jumping on a motorcycle and starting to ride among the buildings.

"I can't believe it!" I say while removing the VRM slowly. I see Jollya has removed the glasses already, and surprisingly Camelos is leaning against the wall, looking at me with his cold green eyes while a smile is drawn on his filthy face.

“You crazy foolish man!” I rush toward him, and just when I approach him with my fist, I punch the air and he just disappears.

“You missed, as always,” he says, standing behind me.

“What are you?”

“I’m the one who saved your wife and—”

“Finley, not now!” Jollya shouts, interrupting.

“So, Finley . . .” I say before I come at Jollya full of anger.

“You knew that he caused all of that just to satisfy his grudge against our government, and you still deal with this traitor?” I’m getting closer to Jollya’s face, shouting. “We all know that everything was depending on the damn internet, so he shut down the whole system to create chaos in our lives. Jollya! Don’t you understand?” I continue.

“No, you don’t know anything . . .” she says with tears on her cheeks.

“What do you mean?”

She comes to me to give me a hug, and so fast after she wraps her hands around my shoulder, I hold her hands and I see the needle in the left one.

“Jollya, Jollya, it’s crystal clear what you are. You betrayed our country by dealing with a terrorist like this guy, and you . . . and you betrayed Nopoly by sneaking inside the city to get me outside for no reason but hearing that scamp Finley’s tragedy,” I say, holding her hands so tight that they might break at any moment.

Suddenly, someone from behind gives me a pinprick. It was him; I know it from the voice which is telling me:

"Get away from her, Harley!"

With a giddy head, blurred vision, and depleted strength, I wake up looking at Jollya and Finley, who have carried me to a chair. I heard them talking but I was totally numb; now all I hear is my heartbeat drumming in my ears.

I wake up after they've tied me to the chair; and when I start shouting to untie me, they put the VRM on my face again. Everything turns black; in any case, I close my eyes to avoid seeing anything those monsters want me to see.

"I'll help you, Daddy . . ." I hear after a while, so I open my eyes to see who said that; that little voice is coming from a little girl who is standing at a distance holding a candle in this darkness. She gets closer and tries to untie me; I'm moving my hands to help her, and it works. I'm finally free, but the little girl glitchily disappears in a second to appear again at an open door far away from me, but this time without the candle. I remember every time I put the VRM on my eyes, I see the same damn door, but I do follow the light as always to satisfy my curiosity.

When I reach the little girl, who has moved herself to the other side, she disappears in a twinkle, and Jollya is glitchily appearing instead; she turns to touch my cheek before I get a blinding flash that takes me to a running screen in a very dark room after a little glitchy image.

Suddenly, the door of the room is opened so fast by two people who have motorcycle helmets covering their faces, and they get inside in a hurry.

"Congratulations, Finley. You did it! There is no power or internet service anymore. We made it!"

“Thank you Jollya. Is everything ready? Perfect; let the game begins,” Finley says, taking off his helmet.

I’m pretty sure that I’m in Jollya’s memory now, but what was she doing there with this psychopath?! Where was I?!

“I made it thanks to you and the Free Ones who are dispersed around America to finish this operation.

“Free Ones?” and just as I say that I’m taken to a dark place full of people and screens. A man with a mask on his face is standing on the stage talking about something called the Small Changers.

“In the name of our Sibling Bond, and for all the pain we have in our hearts, we will change our situation. America is our country, not our prison! So, on the first of January of 2078, we are all going to launch the Nano Rockets, which will contain our way to escape from the prison we have been put in unwillingly.

“The Super-Nano Ants, under project the Small Changers, is officially ready,” he says and the crowd start applauding. When the crowd fall silent, the man with the mask continues:

“Look at the board to see the technology that will be used in the Super-Nano Ants.

“So, this is our beautiful Nano Ant, small creatures with a very special body. With only a two-hundred-and-fifty-micrometer size, it can fit anywhere without being seen; what would be scarier than something they can’t see, hah?”

The noise of the crowd starts to increase as they shout:

“Nothing!”

“Yeaah, haha. Look at this little one. This ant’s effect will be so huge, unlike its size; this Nano Ant will stop the electricity by consuming it, and after that, it'll crash all kinds of electromagnetic waves and radio waves. It can send reflective waves at the speed of light from its body. So, guess what is going to happen when about fifty quadrillion—it's a very huge number—of these little tiny things fly through the atmosphere everywhere in this blessed country? Pooff! Before the fireworks explode in the sky, Nano Ants will be released to spread everywhere and crash this system; the system that makes you suffer by forcing you to live separated from the other social classes."

"Yaaaaa!" they all scream and applaud like apes while I'm screaming:

"Nooo!" I'm shocked by this evil and inhumane idea. This nano thing could be very dangerous!

I get back to that black room with a quick glitch, looking at this Finley through the eyes of my treacherous wife and cursing them both.

"Now, let's connect to Times Square please . . ." he says, looking at me, or Jollya maybe.

After a while, the blue screen fills with numbers, and Finley is preparing himself for something.

"Happy New Year, America! My name is Camelos, and today is a big day for us. I'm shutting down the power with the internet for a while, so don't get in a panic over stopping your streams for a couple of hours, days, or maybe years; it depends on the government's response. Call me on my only active radio frequency (381.1475.18) to contact me directly. Anyway, how are you, people?" Finley says confidently.

I can see through the screens how the panic is taking hold of everyone in Times Square with the darkness which hangs over them.

"Sorry, but our Central Intelligence Agency wants to talk to me privately," he says, smiling.

"What is this?" a deep voice responds from the screen.

"I'm really glad that you were the first to start talking to me personally . . ."

"Who is this?"

"Call me Camelos."

"What have you done? And what do you want?"

"Listen carefully to what I'm about to say! You are not in a position to investigate me. All you need to know is that I'm the one responsible for all of that, and I have full individual control over YOU."

"What is your evidence that you are the only one responsible?"

"I'll let you contact our hidden government to discuss the conditions that I have if you want me to turn the power and the internet service on again."

"How are we going to contact them?"

"In my special way, it's called Nanonet." And he laughs hysterically before continuing, "You can't do anything without the Internet, can you?

"Now, use this frequency to contact the government (5.229.12), and use the last frequency to reach me again," Finley ends, hanging up.

A glitchy image comes back, showing Finley sitting and writing something on a piece of paper, and he receives a call.

"We are amazed at how you did that; can you tell us the process when we have you here working with the Central Intelligence Agency for a very high salary?"

"My sense of humanity prevents me from telling the secret. And no thank you; I don't want to be part of privacy hackers," Finley responds ungratefully.

"One hundred million; is it enough?"

"Nah . . ."

"Two hundred million . . ."

"More!" this filthy man negotiates, laughing!

"Three hundred and fifty million!"

"Why so stingy?"

"Five hundred, and this is the number we can ask the government for . . ."

"How much is a human life worth? Oh, let me guess . . . nothing in your calculations, but in mine: one human life is worth all lives in this Earth. And now, we can negotiate; how many lives have we ended from the fifteenth century until now? Answer me and I'm yours."

"Many, I suppose . . . So, what is your request?"

"To save what is left of humanity." Finley goes silent and then continues, "To have the internet back before you lose more millions of dollars and billions of pieces of information you need to continue controlling, three things need to be done."

"What are they?"

“First, get rid of all nuclear weapons, warheads, rockets, and bombs by sending them into the vacuum of space, and I’ll have to check that we don’t have even one nuke firework in this land.

“After that, the Dastro program must be shut down forever by letting me hack it and destroy it from the inside; I’ll do that to maintain the privacy of all the information in its database. And that means getting back to our old-school system that we had more than three decades ago.

“Last but not least, the government must sign an agreement to ensure the right of the Inferios and the Outferios rights: all the politicians in the government have to be changed for elected politicians from the American population; the changing will occur also to the rules that support the isolation of the poor class from the rest, the limbs trade, and experiments on humans.”

“Are you out of your damn mind? These things can’t be changed in this way and that easily!” the man from the CIA roars.

“How many lives have to be ruined to change this scrap system?” Finley responds emotionally.

“In the public interest, we will do anything—”

“Public! What about the other millions of Americans who are living at rock bottom because of some politicians’ decisions?” Finley interrupts.

“You know that it’s not going to help you to hide wherever you are, and you’ll be caught now or later.”

“You are nothing without the internet; you can’t even find your mom’s address without it!”

"You know that your country, our country will be in danger in such a situation as this. Are you waiting till Russia attacks us all of a sudden?"

"That's why I gave you my requests, and it's up to you now. Take your time talking to your hidden government; and oh, I almost forgot to tell you that this conversation wasn't private this time," Finley ends before hanging up.

I'm shocked, speechless, and full of anger at that stupid Finley because this is not the way to fix the problems: by creating another one.

A glitchy image comes quickly, showing me another picture of Finley sitting and crossing his arms.

"Can you hear me, Mr. Camelos?"

"I can. Can you hear me Mr. President?"

"Yeah, I do hear you . . ."

"That's sad, because you couldn't before this crisis Mr. President."

"So, you know that you made a crisis for the USA . . ."

"No; actually, it's a crisis for all papermakers. Any good news, president?"

"Nothing . . . No one can control the USA government in this way."

"Nothing? No one! Are you sure?"

"Sending all nuclear weapons is just a stupid thing to do. How are we going to protect our country and nation from any attack? We have our respect in the whole world and we'll not lose it at any cost, Camelos."

"I know that it's not that important for you to check social media and see how the people are making fun of you, but I'm quite sure that the electricity is the nerve center for our economy, industry, and military. And you may know how important the internet is for the FBI, CIA, and the other agencies, right?"

"You're crazy!" and the president just hangs up.

After a few seconds, Finley receives another call from the CIA, so he responds:

"Welcome back."

"We are going to press the government to fulfill all your requests, but if you break your promise to bring the power and internet back, it will be war."

"Just to let you know, I'm going to do the same thing with Russia and the other nuke countries, so we'll not be the only country clear from the nuclear weapons—"

"Okay, we'll contact you soon." And the CIA ends the call.

Finley seems confident, especially when he receives the CIA's call again.

I'm getting sick and tired of these glitchy images; but I really want to see how this negotiation will end, hopefully by catching this madman.

"Hello again, beautiful CIA!"

"We have discussed the request, and it looks like you have good intentions. We don't really need nuclear weapons if the whole world will get rid of these kinds of destructive weapons . . ."

“Wow; that’s a legendary speech from you. Honestly, I didn’t expect that from you,” Finley says, laughing after he pauses the call.

“But we need the electricity to start with the first request. And you have to turn the internet on again to continue the rest of your requests . . .”

“You convinced the government that easily; I’m amazed actually!”

“You don’t know how much we stand to lose in all sectors, especially our security one, which is the most harmed . . .”

“If you break the promise, I’ll make you all stop breathing.” Finley is directly threatening the CIA; what the hell! And the CIA is accepting the deal! I’m done.

Finley Chalker

13- Losing Control

I scream and scream, calling Jollya and asking her to free me from this endless pain. The traitorous Jollya removes the VRM, showing me her fake tears and saying:

"Honey, you—"

"Do not call me that. For me, our marriage is done, and you are—" Jollya is covering my mouth with her hand, stopping me from talking, while that foolish Finley is looking at the ground and crossing his arms.

"You need to see what you've missed, otherwise you'll be lost in anger. Watch and analyze, and then decide . . ." she says, shedding tears and touching her head with mine.

"Just get away from me," I respond, moving my head away from hers; and she puts the glasses on my face again.

A quick glitch takes me to the negotiation room again, where everyone in the room is astonished.

"They are really launching them!" Finley says, almost jumping out of his chair.

"Look at this! Thousands of rockets and missiles are starting to be unleashed. Look at the astonished people too!" Jollya, who I'm seeing through her eyes by the VRM, says to Finley, pointing to the four screens in front of her.

"People seem so glad, haha!" the lady, who was with Finley in the car, says.

"You made it! I'm . . . I'm speechless!" Jollya responds.

“Wait a minute! There’s something wrong with this story!” I scream, but obviously, I can’t hear myself.

A few seconds later the VRM is removed from my eyes, and that damn Finley is looking at me directly asking:

“What’s wrong?”

“How could you contact them by radio if there is no signal for the electromagnetic or radio waves? And how could you film these scenes, you liar?”

“Nice question, but bad attitude. My Super-Nano Ants are super for a reason; these ants are so tiny but every single one of them can reflect the waves ten centimeters around it. Let’s say there were more than fifty quadrillion of them flying everywhere, covering America to fifty kilometers up, and all of them are sending crashing waves. The amazing thing about these things is that they have an ability besides their job, and it is to act as radio and electronic transformers; you get me?”

“How . . . how did you get such numbers of these things?”

“To cut a long story short. I had friends in the Chosen Class because I was pretending that I was one of them, and because of that, I could finance scientists in a group I’ve created called the Free Ones; these scientists were doing much research to find a solution that could possibly change our system.

“One day, our scientists found a type of invertebrate animal that lives inside dead human bodies. These creatures, which look like ants, showed strange behavior when fed burning fluorine, such as enjoyment in eating the electricity, and when they did so, they started to send very long waves, which didn’t affect the living cells, but they destroyed all kinds of electromagnetic and radio waves around them. As soon as I heard of that discovery, I bought every single cemetery in Delaware.

"A friend of mine called Nicola, who was from the Chosen Class, has scrap metals, so I asked him to give me all the liquids that come from the burning metals. He thought I was using them for my art, but the reality is I was taking these liquids to extract the fluorine to feed these Nano Ants that were inside the dead bodies in the cemeteries that I had."

"You used dead bodies for your filthy project! What a monster!" I respond emotionally.

"This monster is a master in humanity, unlike your politicians.

"For your information, all the dead bodies had to be burned according to the law (to save the graves as places to be invested in something else). So, I used their dead bodies just before they got burned."

"Even though, you had to ask their families at least to . . ."

"To destroy your perfect system," he finishes my sentence.

"Wasn't it better to use all your money to help your pathetic people?"

"Could I? For more than twenty million poor unlucky Outferios and hundred million of Inferios?! In the best way, I paid for the workers and the scientists in my little secret company." He smiles, winking at me.

"You are—"

"In conclusion, I used the dead bodies of the humans and the robots; so, just guess the number of deaths of both of them. End of story." Before he covers my eyes with the glasses, he looks at me with a cold, scary look.

A damn glitchy image confuses my vision, and I get back to the darkroom with Finley and the other assistant.

"Fifteen thousand missiles have been launched," the CIA says.

"It takes you six hours! I ate my favorite cuisine while seeing the real fireworks flying through our sky," Finley says, laughing.

"Turn them on, quickly!"

"Patience! I just want to make sure that all these nasty weapons will head into space—"

"Didn't you check every single nuke central? The last batch of missiles has been sent. We need to be connected with the world now!"

"Okay, easy boys! I will, I will," Finley responds while working on his own laptop.

"Hurry up please!"

Suddenly, Finley jumps with happiness, and Jollya laughs with tears in her eyes, making my vision blurry.

"What is happening, Camelos? What about the promise you gave us?"

"Wait . . . why have the rest of the missiles changed their direction away from space?" Finley asks but gets no response. "DON'T YOU HEAR ME?!"

"The president is speaking. Camelos, we have just sent at least a hundred of our missiles to your country—"

"WHAT?!"

"Yes, we did sacrifice five thousand in space, hoping to have everything back to its normal situation before finding you, but it didn't work. So, ten thousand missiles will take a journey around the earth to hit all our enemies, and your country will be one of them for sure."

"Whaa . . . WHAT DO YOU MEAN! I'm American, and I live in this damned land!" Finley shouts hysterically.

"Unfortunately, it's your fault because it was a national threat. We didn't lose a war before, nor the control, but if the US falls, the whole miserable world has to fall too . . ."

"You are anti-human people! I can't believe it! ARE YOU DUMB?! The whole world will freaking attack us back!"

"We have our ways to continue living. Get rotted!" And the president hangs up, leaving Finley slumped on the chair, and with wide eyes he says:

"The Third World War has just started . . ."

Jollya gets on her knees, putting her hands on her face to cover the sight.

"You stupid idiot! How didn't you expect that? You have become a murderer of your own folk! Let me free! I WANT TO KILL YOU SO BAD!" I start screaming and shaking myself like crazy. It feels like my head will explode.

"Jollya, Cecelia, go to the Hidden Home, now!"

"And what about you, Finley? What are you going to do?" the assistant, Cecelia, wonders.

"I'll bring everything back to make contact with all target countries . . ."

"But—"

"Please, both of you just go! I'm responsible, and I'll take the risk with this to fix the situation. Go now!" he interrupts Jollya insistently.

After a dramatic pause, Jollya and Cecelia open a heavy door and go inside a metro.

A glitchy image breaks the dread atmosphere in the metro to bring the most horrific thing I've ever heard. The ground is shaking so much that no one can stand up straight, and the explosives seem like they'll never end, so the whole metro is shaking too.

"STOP!" I scream with all my might, and the VRM is taken off my eyes.

"Damn you! Untie me! I swear I'm going to kill you. And you Jollya, I don't know what to tell you. You betrayed me to be with this scum . . . Eh."

She starts crying for no reason, but I don't care about her fake tears anymore. I'd never believe her . . . never.

"I'll free you, and I'll let you choose to know the reason that made her did that, or not. But you have to know that you have such a powerful wife—"

"SHUT THE HELL UP, AND FREE ME NOW!"

Jollya stands up from her chair, takes the scissors by force from the devil, and gets closer to me, looking into my eyes, which are telling her how much I hate her.

"Harley, you should know that I love you . . . forever . . ."

I don't want to respond to her lies, so I point with my eyes to my tied hands.

As soon as she unties me, I stand up and get Jollya out of my way after taking the scissors from her by force.

"You don't deserve to be alive at this point, Piggy."

"I don't?!"

I'm running toward That Finley after his cold response with a pair of scissors ready to shred his face, but just when the edge of the scissors touches him, he disappears.

"I know that you are a coward, but the hologram will not stop me from ending your filthy life, Piggy," I shout, looking everywhere, ignoring the terrified Jollya. And then, I turn to Jollya who is frozen in place.

"WHY?! What made you do that to me, to us?!" I pull her with my right hand by her jacket. "We were living together in prosperity, and you know how much I loved you. But what did I get in return? This . . ." I continue, waving with my cyber hand that is holding the scissors and pointing to the place we were in, before I let her hand.

"Why did you show me all of that? Why did you even take me out of freaking Nopoly?

"For two reasons; do you want to know them before your hate consumes the wrong ones?" that damn voice comes behind me; slowly, I turn my head, responding:

"NO! I don't want anything from you, but killing you." And I look back to Jollya, assuming that he is just a hologram and intending not to follow this mirage; but as soon as I know where the real Finley is, I'll not let him live, I promise.

"The first one is to use your fancy mask—"

"I said NO!" I shout in front of Jollya's face, and she gently pushes me away from her. I decide to go away from my unfaithful wife, and I walk slowly to him hoping he is the real one, and ask:

"Use my mask! For what?!"

"So, you want me to talk now; okay then. We needed your VI mask to hack it and take all the information in its memory, so thank you!"

"Hacking, again! Interesting. What is the other reason?" and I get closer to him.

"Yes, which leads us to the second reason, which is this little girl and the other kids . . ." Finley says holding a picture for a little girl.

I freeze in my place while I'm burning from inside; that girl I'm looking at concerns me. I fall down with so many flashback memories and a horrible noise in my ears, and I start crying like a little kid. I don't feel anything, not even the time that I spend crying on my knees with a bent body and a head on the floor.

"Where is she?!" I try to scream with my broken voice while my tears are blinding me.

"Get up, and continue recovering the most important part of your memory. And don't worry, Lori is alive," Finley says, and then he gives me a hand to stand up on my feet. I feel so lost with a frozen dizzy brain and a wet face. "I'm the real one, Harley. Do you want to go on with the memory journey, or kill this piggy? It's really your choice now," he continues.

"Lori . . ." I say with so much sadness in my voice, taking the VRM from Jollya after a warm hug from her, and then she sits again on her chair with the machine on her head.

The first thing I see is a running kid from afar; I try to follow this kid because she could be . . . How did I lose her? What is happening with her now?

After a few seconds, everything turns crazy. The walls become paintings with a childish look, and then they turn to scary dark pictures; I hear her voice screaming behind the same door that has always existed in my VRM journey, but this time, it's closed; so I throw myself into it to push it and open this damn door. Why is it a locked door?

"Why?" I scream before I feel a little hand pulling my hand from behind.

"It's you, my little angel! Where have you been?" I ask her before she disappears. I turn around again to the door, which has opened slightly. After getting inside, I watch Jollya just standing there so lonely, so I come to her; and when I touch her, I start seeing through her eyes again.

The place reminds me of our home. It is actually our home with all the old-style stuff that Jollya loved, like the dream catcher, the Egyptian eye, and so many other things. Jollya is walking through the house, and I remember how much I loved this place, which has piece of memories in every inch of it. She continues walking till she approaches a colorful room full of paintings of very old cities.

"Hello, beauty. Mommy is here," and she gives me a hug with a kiss on the cheek.

"What a beautiful picture, baby Lori. As I can see, this is an old town, right? Is it in the United States? Is it?" And Lori signals yes before she receives a hug from Jollya. "Oh, my lovely girl." Jollya continues hugging her while my angel is painting.

"I know that you are hearing Mommy, and Mommy wants to tell you that she loves you . . ."

"Mom, Mommy . . ."

"Yes, honey! Mommy is with you, here, always and forever," Jollya says, pointing to Lori's little heart with the palm of her hand.

"Song . . . song . . ." Lori keeps repeating, moving her head unstably. And Jollya takes a breath before starting:

"*I'm looking straight into your eyes,*

Telling you how much you are nice

Such a little cute doll,

With a beautiful pure soul

***

Hush, little Lori, I'm here don't worry

Deep in my heart, I put you with your daddy

Draw line by line the beauty inside you,

Sing with me like an angel 'I love you'

Be wherever, I'm always with you,

And together, yeah together, and forever for you

We are here together, and forever

Nothing is better, for now and ever, my lovely little angel

***

All these noises you hear,

They are from the song I sing, my dear

I know it's sometimes hard to believe,

That I'm here, but someday you'll achieve

To remember all the kisses I give

With all the hugs that you receive

Because I will keep giving you more till you can't count them all

Let the god bless you, and live in peace,

Close your eyes and see your mommy, please

Everyone will know how much I love you,

In your tiny heart, surely you know that too

All I do to show you how much Daddy and Mommy love you,

And we won't leave you, no, no

Together and forever we will live, love, laugh forever and together

***

Be wherever, I'm always here inside,

And together, yeah together, keep that in your mind

We are always together, yeah forever,

And together, nothing is better, for now and ever, my lovely little angel

***

I'm looking straight into your eyes,

Telling you how much you are nice

Such a little cute doll, with a beautiful pure soul"

Jollya ends the song that I remember was for Lori.

“What a beautiful song!” someone with a voice nearly the same as mine says from behind.

Jollya turns to see . . . me behind her! It’s so confusing to see myself through my wife’s eyes. And now, I have another point of confusion because the song sounds so familiar; I heard this melody in the Temple!

“Hello, darling; how was work?”

“It was good. Are you ready?”

“Harley, are you sure it’s a good idea to let them try the medicine on our daughter?”

“We are running out of choices, and this is our last hope; hopefully, it will treat her autism.”

A glitchy image takes us to a doctor in a clinic, who says:

“We’ve tested the medicine, and it seems to have side effects, so we have to put Lori under observation when she has the medicine. The good news is that the potential to cure autism with this medicine is great. So, let’s give it a chance, shall we?”

“Can I discuss this with my husband in private, please?”

“Sure; take your time. I’ll bring you a cup of coffee.” And the doctor leaves, closing the door.

“Harley, I don’t feel good about this, it’s just wrong to test medicine on our daughter. I’m just hoping that she’ll recover.”

“What choice do we have?”

“I don’t feel we’re doing the right thing for Lori,” Jollya says, crying and rubbing her eyes to dry her tears.

The discussions continue between me and Jollya about the subject for a long time, but a knock on the door ends the discussion.

"Excuse me, but are you done discussing?"

"Ye . . . yeah, sure Doctor Felix, we've decided to give it a chance," I say.

"It's a hard decision, and I appreciate your trust. We'll take Lori to room 8, and there you can visit her any time."

"Can I stay with her? Please!"

"Sorry ma'am, but we can't leave you with her during the therapy time . . ."

Suddenly, all the lights turn off, and everyone is disappearing, but I hear someone is crying, begging someone. I run to the door I used to go through every time I'll see through someone's eyes, but this time it is worn and broken. I get inside it, and there's a blinding flash before I see myself with a sad, shocked face looking at the doctor screaming:

"WHAT?! HOW DID THAT HAPPEN?!"

"I understand your feelings Mr. Harley, but her heart couldn't tolerate the medicine. I'm really sorry for what happened to her . . ."

"Please I need to see her at least . . ." Jollya says, crying on my shoulder.

"We can't let you see her in that state, so please, understand the situation . . ."

"I WILL SUE YOU, ALL OF YOU!" I scream at the doctor, and I do remember this horrible event that is engraved in my memory; how could I forget that she is dead? But Finley says she's alive! Why would he—

"Sir, you've signed on the papers that you are responsible for the decision you have taken about the therapy!"

"You know what? I have a better idea . . ." and I hit the doctor in the face and go crazy, hitting everyone wearing a white suit and black shoes. But after I lose control of myself, the police come and take me out of there with my all tears and my wife, who looks an emotional wreck.

14- Different Perspective, Different Story

A long blinding flash is running across my vision, making me feel depressed, lonely, and lost, which I believe were Jollya's feelings at that time. Then, in a blink of an eye, I get back to our dark, cold, lifeless home where Jollya is packing a black bag, so I'm still seeing through her eyes; and at the speed of light with a quick glitch, I end up in a place where Finley is sitting at his computer.

"Finn, I need your help . . ." Jollya begins.

"I did help you, and you do remember what Harley responded when I tried to help. The healer, who I led you to, is still in prison! For doing what?"

"Look, it was really dumb what Harley did to him when he was only helping Lori in . . . his spiritual way, I know that already, and I paid his family for all the damages—"

"Well, thank you! but the financial compensation can't cover the psychological damage to his children and his wife . . ." Finley interrupts emotionally.

I do remember that old man who was trying to help Lori by reading something from a religious book which, personally, I didn't think could help; and that old man was nothing but a crook.

"That help let me know my stepbrother, and I was always grateful for knowing such a good man like you."

"Yeah, thanks to the 'A Hand 4 U' site . . ." And he laughs a small laugh.

"Finley, I've lost everything now: my man, and my daughter; would you leave your sister in this state?"

Finley sighs a long sigh, and then responds:

"What do you want me to do?"

"All I want is to see my daughter before your burial company burns her little body and buries her ashes."

Finley sighs and looks at the ground before he looks again at Jollya, saying in a low sad tone:

"I'll let Future Trees contact me when they receive the body. I'm sorry for what happened to Lori . . ."

A flash takes me to when Jollya is holding a necklace that has a little picture in it of Lori, crying when a random guy knocks at the open door and says:

"Finley wants to talk to you." And she runs hysterically, screaming: "Have you found her?!"

"I have . . ." Finley says with astonishment on his face.

"Where?!"

"After a huge search and many hacking operations on the system of the hospital that Lori was in, I found hidden documents and evidence that this hospital works secretly with a company called BioID."

"BioID! . . . what?!"

"It's a company that takes care of the development of human beings by doing experiments on them . . ."

"And how does this relate to our issue?"

"Read for yourself!" And he opens a window on the computer.

"Project OC22

We are seeking a pure mind that can create a whole complete and fine world. This brain is required to be young and fresh.

Take your time and contact us as soon as you find this brain.

BioID

09/09/2070"

"So, what does that mean?"

"Look at the response from the hospital, sister."

"About project OC22

We have discovered another brain that you requested on 09/09/2070. The person who has the requirements you asked for is younger than the others.

The girl is two and a half years old and has autism, and this girl has such an immense imagination, which is reflected in the pictures she draws that have very old-fashioned touches in them.

The parents have brought us the girl to be treated, so you'd better hurry up before they change their minds.

Sharon Hospital

Delaware

18/10/2074"

Jollya is shocked, and so am I. Silence hangs over the place, but Jollya breaks it saying:

"They took her to conduct experiments on her!"

"It's clear that they will do so. At least we know that she is alive . . ."

"How can we get Lori back?"

"There is no straight legal way because BioID is funded by a very clean politician: Keres Pessinger," Finley says ironically.

I have to admit, Keres was the worst human living on Earth; he was encouraging every war that would kill as many as possible because he was thinking that weak folks weren't needed.

"Have you tried to get into the system of this BioID company?" Jollya asks with a broken voice.

"We don't have much time to hack their hard system, but I have a better plan to get your daughter back. All I need to know is the building plan of BioID, and it's easy to find . . ."

"Where is this company? Is it so far away from here?"

"This company has at least one branch in every state in the US, so we'll head to the one in Delaware, hoping that she is there . . ."

A blink of Jolly's eyes takes me to a bunch of people who are face-covered.

"This is the Sacqer Squad, who will bring your daughter back today; right guys?" Finley says confidently.

"YES SIR!" the group shouts as one.

"Let's go, let's go!" They rush while they're getting inside their colorful cars to move on.

A glitch plays in my vision, taking me to a little beautiful room; it is Lori's room. I'm sitting and Lori is on my lap; she is just fine! But the damn glitch takes me away from her to Finley's place again! What does this man want now?

"Finn, I want to tell you something very important . . ."

"Well hello sis, have a seat."

"Yeah, thank you. So, what are you doing these days?"

"I'm just working on something . . ."

"And that is . . .?"

"Don't worry about it. You need to take care of little Lori" he says, smiling.

"Finley, you helped me many times and you were always behind my back . . ., but this time, I really want to help with everything I have. Look, you have to trust me because I'm fully trusting you, and that's why I want to offer you all the money I have to do . . . whatever it takes to end this madness, please. I got my daughter back, but there are other kids and people who are suffering somehow because of this whole crazy system."

"Dry your tears because I was planning on it, and I'll start it now . . ." Finley responds, jumping out of his chair. "But first, how much do you have?" he continues, doing the gesture of counting money in his hand.

"Twenty-six . . ."

"This can afford you a meal from Hungry XL with extra French fries," he says, laughing.

"Million, Mr. Finley." Jollya is trying to hide her laughter.

"I'm just joking, haha. That's perfect to start the Small Changers project."

"I want just one last thing . . ."

"Tell me!" Finley responds after sighing.

"Lori won't be happy living without her father, and . . . and I know that seems impossible, but seeing my daughter alive, thanks to you, will change Harley forever, and he would probably charge you more money; ten times more than I have, hopefully . . ."

"And you want to stay here forever!"

"If that doesn't bother anyone . . ." Jollya says, and Finley starts laughing.

"What's so funny, Fin?"

"You feel safe to live here with your family, where all the wealthy people get afraid to cross our places, rather than living in the civilized areas with all their security! Now that is funny to me," he responds, smiling.

"I know exactly what you mean, but this is not a place of Outferios; it's a place of the humble, nice, kind, and unfortunate people who live unfairly in this unfair world . . ."

"But fortunately, we have good people like you highlighting that. Thank you, Jollya!" And he calls his men:

"We have a monkey to release from his cage . . ."

"Finley! This monkey would be my husband!"

"He is the kind of person who believe in evolution, and that means his predecessors were monkeys, so basically he is—"

"I got it, please stop it!" Jollya, my love, responds.

"The monkey would thank you for all of this, piggy . . ." I say after removing my VRM.

"For what? Everything I did for my sister, her lovely daughter, and even for her money was motivated by humanity . . ."

"She is not your sister, okay? But thank you anyway."

"I and Jollya have the same father, so that makes us neighbors, right?" Finley says ironically. "You're welcome anyway . . ."

"Oh, okay . . . So, where is Lori now? Why haven't I seen her yet?" I'm wondering, smiling.

"Honey, there is an important part because you didn't accept to move out of the Chosen Class, after the lawyer Mitsue got you out of the prison," Jollya points out while she is sitting on the chair.

I get a sudden pain in my stomach, and it doesn't feel good at all; but I put the VRM on with my shaking hands waiting for the weird vision and the creepy door that always exist in the beginning of my memories journey, but neither of those appear; instead, I'm standing in the middle of a park full of beautiful colored flowers, flying butterflies, and running pure water everywhere around me.

"Is this the heaven that all the religious talk about?" I say, looking at this work of art around me.

"No dad, we are not!" a little voice comes from behind, so I look behind me to see my Lori; I open my arms waiting for her to run to me and give me a hug, but she runs away instead . . .

"Lori! Why are you running from Daddy? I miss you so much, don't you miss me?" Lori signs yes, crying.

"Forgive me, baby . . .I . . ." I try to justify something from all the wrong things I've done, but I'm totally lost for words. The worst thing is that I wasn't able to remember her without this VRM.

I head to the door that I was waiting for by following my little angel, who gets inside and closes it. The door is firmly closed, so I come closer to it to open it and get inside Jollya's eyes, probably. Just before the door opens, it explodes into flames, throwing me back roughly.

"NO! Loooriii!" I scream, struggling to get up to run after my disappeared daughter. The flame is consuming the door, but I'll not give a damn about going through it at all; and I do it. I feel the flame burning my skin so that it becomes darker and darker. I come up with a theory now that says: We can be any color, but we still have the same feelings of sadness, anger, happiness, and pain.

The pain I feel now is equal to someone's else pain, but all my feelings are now freezing when a glitch takes me to the painful scene that Jollya saw. I'm watching Lori being taken from my wife's hands by force in the middle of the destroyed buildings (the place we lived in, after the nuke crisis as I remember). In the middle of the fight between the stubborn mom and the soldiers who have gas masks on their faces, she gets a gunshot. I don't remember something like that, Jollya getting shot there! Where was I at that time? I would kill them all without any mercy . . .

The vision becomes clear when Jollya opens her eyes in a dark and wet place that seems to be in Dallecus.

"What just happened?" Jollya says with dizzy vision.

"Don't worry, sister; you are in safe . . ." someone, who is blurry, says.

"Wh . . . where is Lo . . ." she's trying to speak, coughing in pain.

"Relax! She'll be safe too . . ."

"Did she get a shot?!" Jollya is freaking out.

"No, no! You need to rest now because you have lost a lot of blood," the man says.

Jollya is closing her eyes, and that blinds me for a while, before I see that disheveled and blue-eyed man with a nasty radiation suit. That man who was wealthy and finely dressed, who has fallen to this terrible state now, is me. But a flash appears to end this vision and takes me to an untidy dark room.

"It was a bad idea objecting to living here . . . and leaving you with Lori to find the water was the worst idea," I say, shedding a tear.

"We all make mistakes," Jollya says, holding my hand, and continues, "Harley, look . . . do you remember when I was telling you that I have to visit Monica?"

"Your friend, who was so very sick and in need of you. Tell me, what are you hiding, Jollya?"

"Promise me . . . Promise me to keep calm and not get mad about me or anyone else!"

"Talk Jollya, please!"

She sighs before she breathes out, saying:

"I was going to Monica, but . . ."

"BUT WHAT?!"

“Monica wasn’t sick, she wasn’t my friend either . . .” she says, holding my hand there, but I take my hand away from hers. I suppose that I was mad at her at that moment, as am I now.

“Since Finley tried to help Lori and then released her from that company, and after helping me to be with you after everything you did to his friend . . .” and she goes silent.

“Carry on . . .”

“I removed my real IDD at that time to work with Finley, and Monica was nothing but an assistant to him. Finley was working on a super-secret project called ‘the Small Changers,’ and I was coming to help him with this project; that’s why I called you just before the attack, telling you to get yourself and Lori to the panic room.”

“You mean he was the one responsible for this whole situation!”

“Wait, Harley!” Jollya is calling me, coughing.

“I’ll kill this scum . . .” stupid me says, leaving.

“No, Harley, come back here; I need you . . .” but Harley doesn’t come back; why did I do that? Was my anger bigger than my love for her? All these questions are fading now when I hear myself roaring outside of Jollya’s room, asking:

“WHERE IS FINLEY? WHERE IS HE?”

Jollya is trying to get up, but the bullet wound has left her in pain, so she is struggling to make a simple movement. At that moment, everything I saw through Jollya’s memory is running so fast across my sight, and once I see Lori fading away, that makes me cry and cry till I feel my tears are dropping from my face; so I remove the VRM to get back the present and say something I never thought I'd say.

"Lori, I'm . . . I'm sorry sweetheart. Jollya, I'm so sorry my love," I say, kneeling and crying; she bows herself too to accommodate this despicable human hugging her.

After a while, I get up with my lovely Jollya, and I decided to do it after drying my tears.

"Finley, I'm sorry man . . ."

"God forgives everyone, so why don't we do that?" he responds, smiling with glittery eyes.

"And thank you . . ." I put my hands over my eyes, feeling the pain in my head.

"Honey, are you alright?"

"I just feel dizzy; I'm okay. So, tell me what did I do to you Finley, after I got mad?"

"Your anger makes you fallen, my friend . . ." Finley answers instead of Jollya.

"What do you mean?"

"You've been taken to the Utopia, Nopoly."

"Did they take the rest of the men?"

"Not all of them . . ." Jollya responds.

"Why did they take me then?"

"The answer is in your VI mask, which we broke its system to take all the information from its memory, Mr. Cooper!" Finley utters, smiling.

"Ah, my head! I have the worst headache of my life . . ."

“Honey, everything will be okay. Please Finn, don’t press him like this. You told me that we have to help him recover his memory, right?” Jollya says.

“That’s right, and that is what I’m doing now. He gotta remember his life inside the city too!”

“I do . . . Honey, it’s okay; I’m alright,” and I look at Finley with a defeated look.

“What about Lori? Where is she?”

“Inside . . . with the other kids who had been taken from their parents . . .” Finley signals with his head out of the room.

“So, the soldiers belong to that damn Nopoly,” I say looking at the ground, and then I raise my head, continuing, “I have to save her!”

“Calm down! We are going inside Nopoly . . . to save them all . . .” he responds with the biggest, most confident smile I’ve ever seen and eyes full of hope. And, suddenly, this piggy becomes someone I respect.

Jollya Woodman

15- On Our Way to Nopoly

One hundred of the Free Ones have been divided into ten groups under the name Free Rebels, who will enter Nopoly from different places to save the children and take them back to the rest of their families; I, Jollya, Finley, and seven others are in one group; honestly, I don't remember their names, except the big guy, Steven.

Everyone dresses in the proper clothes with the gas masks before going out to the surface.

"Should I be happy or astonished to have you with us, Harley? I don't really know . . ." says Finley, patting my shoulder and smiling a wide smile.

"I was always considering you as an enemy . . ."

"And now?"

"How are we going to get into the city, boss?" I ask him, smiling back.

"Through the dumpsite of the demons' corpses."

"What?!" I'm wondering, so confused.

"We will enter by the place that is used to throw out the dead bodies. From there we can sneak past the gate to the city with a little help from Sam," Finley responds.

"You are out of your mind to have this plan. And who the hell is Sam?"

"You'll meet him there . . . hopefully," Finley points out.

We get out to where the place is totally ruined, destroyed, and full of dead things and beings. The weather reminds me of

Sweden, where I traveled once for business; there was a shy sun which was clouded and snow drizzle, but the difference here is the sun is covered with black-red clouds, and the ashes take its place in the air thanks to the storms.

My thoughts stop with a question from Jollya:

"Honey, are you okay?"

"Why do I remember things only when I see something related to those things? Do you understand me?"

"I do . . . and that was because your memory has been partly cleared."

"When? And by whom?" I ask Jollya, who stops walking. "What's the matter, Jollya?" I continue; but the answer doesn't come because we have just discovered that there is a squad of the ExA in the area. I get angry at the fact we have to watch in silence because we don't have a chance of facing them all, especially given they are fully armored and sticking together. It just feels so awkwardly weak seeing that and not daring to do a thing about it.

"Close your eyes if you can't control your anger."

"But they are taking the little ones!" I respond emotionally to Finley.

"Don't be reckless! They can kill us so easily. Don't you want to save Lori?" He asks me and I answer yes while hitting the ground.

We leave the place for a while, but I'm still thinking about the poor children who were taken to the armored car of the ExA.

"Harley, I did it . . . in Nopoly," Jollya says suddenly.

"Did what, honey?"

"I partly cleared your memory in the city . . ."

"You?! But why, and how?"

Jollya makes no response at first, but then starts talking:

"Do you remember when you got out to find Finley?"

"That was the last scene I watched through the VRM; I do remember . . ."

"I tried to follow you and stop you from getting out, but you didn't listen to me and just went . . ."

"And instead of finding me to get rid of me, the ExA found you first and took you to the boomtown," Finley says scornfully.

"Why didn't they take you or anyone else. Why me, Mr. Fin?"

"As I told you before, many people have been taken too. For those people who had special thoughts before this crisis, a guaranteed trip to Nopoly was confirmed, according to my Search Squads."

"Special thoughts! What does that mean?" I ask him, confused, but Jollya sighs and decides to answer:

"It was a long time ago when you were in the Caucasian Circle Club, which was a hate group that supported only the white when they got in trouble because of racism. This CCC had political agendas that talked about the problems that came with the propagation of the non-white races . . ."

"And they attacked the other nations in the US in the media, accusing them of terrorism and defaulting; the CCC attacked mostly the Outferios and Inferios, or what they called

Lowple," Finley says with deep sadness, before a middle-aged man in the group jumps in saying:

"That's true, but not all of us agreed on those thoughts . . ."

"Exactly, and Harley changed a lot after we started dating, do you remember, honey?" Jollya says, holding my hand.

"I told you before, you are my guardian angel," I respond, and then I whisper to Jollya:

"But you didn't need to tell these parts of my history . . ."

"Haha, we still hear you. My friend, I know so much about you and Nopoly, thanks to your VI mask," Finley says confidently.

"But was I that silly to join this group?"

"You say that because you've seen the consequences. And you don't need to stop walking every time you become shocked. There are more shocking things," Finley replies. I am shocked to hear that there are more than all these crazy things, but I continue walking in my astonishment.

"But what does this have to do with the subject of taking me to Nopoly and clearing my memory by you, Jollya?!"

"Going back to the time you went out to find me and kill me, you had been taken to the city because the government there wanted to build a harmonious society in the utopia Nopoly. And to have been a member of one of the hate groups in the past is enough to make you chosen to be searched by the ExA, and they let you live in a city that contains only the first race with a possibility of making you sight-controlled," Finley clarifies, making me so ashamed.

"But I quit the CCC, why would they take me?"

“There is always a way to raise the devil inside anyone,” Finley says emotionally.

“What do you mean?”

“The fear, Harley . . . the fear . . .” Finley says, and then turns to me continuing:

“If you’ve read history, you’ll see how the fear destroyed Europe in WWI. The fear that Germany had of being besieged by other European countries, the fear of the Russian kingdom losing its power because of the communist revolution, and the fear of Europe of starting another war on the continent. But ironically, all these fears made all these countries make stupid decisions, leading to making their fears become true.”

“Thanks for reminding me of this disaster, but I’m not destroyed by fear!”

“Thanks to Jollya . . .” a young lady says.

“But they are . . .” Finley adds at the same time, pointing to the covered Nopoly.

I start feeling dizzy with the headache again.

“Honey, honey! Are you okay?”

“I just want you to know that I’ll never leave you, baby. And you have to thank me for forgiving you for clearing my memory.” I try to move the discussion away from my weakness.

“No. You have to thank me for choosing the best costume for my gentleman.”

“Was it you?! Haha, I’ve always liked your test in clothes . . . And thank you . . . thank you for being in my life.” I say to my beautiful lady hugging her from the side.

The sky starts raining a black rain before Finley continues, saying:

“Jollya, can you give me the permission to clarify to your husband in this romantic weather?” And she responds, smiling: “Sure!”

“So, let me tell you why and how she cleared your empty head. Well, Jollya followed you out, but while she was running behind you, a squad of ExA, who were busy taking a bunch of kids from their families, watched you—”

“Did they take Jollya?!” I interrupt him.

“Jollya was smarter than to be caught . . .”

“Fin!” Jollya tries to stop him from insulting me, but I signed to her with my hand that it was alright.

“Haha, we are kinda friends now, don’t worry, Jollya.”

“Friends! You’re taking it too far, Finn; but anyway, carry on . . .”

“Where were we? Yes, I remember; so, Jollya watched you from afar planning the next step with Martin, who flowed Jollya to persuade her to get back to Dallecus. Luckily two soldiers from the ExA were a part of the squad, for exploring intentions, right Jollya?”

“Yes, the soldiers were looking for more kids I believe, but unfortunately for them, they got inside the ruined building that I and Martin were hiding in. I was scared, so scared of them seizing me as they did you, and afraid of losing you, so we had no choice but to try to survive by numbing them. The next thing that came to my mind was to use their suits and masks to creep among the ExA, and it succeeded. Playing a male soldier role with the wound that was hurting me wasn't as hard as hearing the others talking about the next exploratory tour . . ."

"How many of them were there?" I ask.

"So many, and they were heavily armed. It killed me when I saw how the soldiers were trying to persuade the parents that their children would be safe with them; and when the family refused to hand over the kids, the ExA found the bullets as a final solution. So . . . the kids and even the young adults were taken by force," says Jollya, crying. "I tried to be the guardian for the prisoners to avoid these inhumane actions," she continues.

"What would be the reason for taking the young and the youth, ignoring the elders?" I question.

"We couldn't find anything related to this subject in your mask, which has only information about the map of the city, your job as a captain in the police, and some important people you have known," Finley says.

"And here comes the memory-clearing part, when I got inside the city with the rest of the ExA and the prisoners. I can't even describe the atmosphere there, but it was really shocking. The system of the city was terrifyingly unique . . . The human beings there were nothing but a tool to use . . ." Jollya's broken voice stops, showing her sadness.

"What do you mean by 'tool'? I was there and life seemed so normal."

"Have you forgotten the VI effect? You'll see for yourself the real city when we get in there.

"Going back to the story, I left the squad telling them I needed to pee, but what I actually did was get inside the section you were taken to, to change the bandage that I had and take some pain relievers. At the beginning, I got freaked when I saw the nurses had something like masquerade masks with wires on their faces and magnifying eyeglasses. I glimpsed you in a room in the section, so I lured a nurse to a place where I could take her outfit and that weird mask; it was called a Recognition Face, which is similar to the VI but shows the real vision to the wearer of it. The RF's job is just to let anyone use the VI to see these nurses and doctors as humans, not demons, according to the books I read in there . . ."

The heavy storm, which is pushing us so hard to the right hand side, stops Jollya from talking.

"Let's hold each others' hands, quickly!" a lady in our group shouts.

We are holding hands, and it feels so different when a number of people put their hands together to survive; this is the first time in my life I feel that feeling. If someone dies, we'll probably all die; if not, there is a chance to live.

A couple of minutes, which feel like hours, pass and the storm calms down, so we continue walking with the radioactive dust that is covering every inch of us.

"That was close . . . good job team, and thanks for the idea, Alexa," Finley says to the lady who replies, "anytime."

"So, back to our story. The same moment I put that RF on my face, after getting rid of the nurse, I knew things I didn't know before. Like who I am, my job, and the details; and all the information flowed to my brain. The RF was connected directly to the cerebrum, and it was sending the information as waves to my brain maintaining free will, also according to what I read."

"That's how they persuaded me with all the ideas I got in the city," I respond to Jollya, and Finley is agreeing: "Correct."

"Seeing you on the chair seized and powerless with all the things that must have been happening to you made me cry, but thankfully, the mask hid my tears.

"My job as a nurse in the Accepting Section was to prepare your brain and eyes to live in Nopoly. It was like a setup of your sight and thoughts to live in the way the Nopoly government wants you to live."

"What about the free will the government bragged about?" Finley asks in disapproval.

"They wanted the freedom that fits their plan, I believe," a young lady says.

"True," Finley and the others agree.

"The important part of the story was the process of erasing your memory, honey. The first step we had to do with the newcomers was to clean their memory totally and replace it with a new one.

"I was thinking about the possibility of escaping with you out of the city, but it was impossible for us, especially with all the soldiers who were outside the room. And the idea of seeing you in that state, powerless and about to lose all your memories of your family, your friends, and yourself, just killed me. But I came up with an idea, which was to limit the things your memory would lose; it was by changing the way of clearing your memory. It was quite hard, especially with another nurse helping me in the room and a camera above us . . ."

"How did you do that, my beautiful intelligent wife?"

Jollya makes no response, maybe she's laughing and trying to hide it, but then she continues:

"Claiming that you had damage to your brain persuaded the other nurse to give me more time to organize the process; but what I did is make you lose your memory partially, and I left the will of free-thinking to you, contrary to what they wanted me to do with you. In the end, the system only needed to see the results in your brain after the operation, and luckily it worked!"

"That explains why I need to see the object to start remembering everything about it . . ." I respond, nodding.

"And I was the first object."

"You're not an object, you are my guardian angel," I say, hugging her.

"I said that because I was Joelle, Jane, Jolly, Joll, and Jollyn who you met in the city, but you probably can't remember all these characters," she adds, laughing.

"I do remember Jollyn and Joll, but I don't have the rest in my mind . . ." I admit, nodding my head.

"You know honey, when you got in the Temple of Science, you had totally forgotten me and what I did to you as Jolly. I think it was a result of deleting the face I had on me in your new memory . . ."

"Why did you do that to me?"

"All the nurses ought to do that for some reason, and that helped me a lot to stop you looking into me when I was trying to get you out of Nopoly. Once, you were so close to arresting me. Thankfully, you had forgotten that face every time you entered the Temple there . . ."

"How many times did you try to take him out of there?" a young man in the group is asking.

"Five times. I used every possible way to make you trust me and follow me to the Accepting Section," Jollya answers.

"Wouldn't it have been easier if you'd untied me and we just ran away?"

"As I told you; you were nearly numbed, and I didn't know anything about how to get out with all the soldiers who were guarding the room. I took advantage of being in the city for a while; I knew so much about the city and how it worked, and I searched for Lori, most importantly."

"It was really brave what you did Jollya, but how could you plan for the escape?" a lady in the group says.

"Thanks, Sena. When I decided to get Harley out, I planned to start the process when all the works ended in Nopoly. But I didn't succeed until Harley believed in me after getting in trouble for using his manners there," Jollya says.

I remembered all the bad things that I lived in the city, and I'm feeling grateful for having Jollya, who I'm looking to saying:

"You know . . . I love you, and I'll love you forever . . ."

"I do love you more than that."

"I believe you," I say while I notice something on Jollya's wrist.

"What is that?" I ask, pointing at it.

"This is the hypnotic needles thrower, and on the other hand is the sleepy thrower; they were really a good proposal from a friend of mine, who used them to escape from the ExA to our underground shelter. She could survive them but not her fiancé . . .”

“Do you mean Keisha’s fiancé who was one of the rare cases of kidnapping?” Finley asks.

“Yes. The lady is African American, and her man is Mexican,” Jollya answers.

“Maybe they were in BBB,” I say ironically, but an African man in our squad, who seems not to like the joke, is jumping and saying aggressively:

“Would you clarify what is BBB?”

“Eeeh . . . Best Black Band, I meant,” I respond, trying to calm him down while Finley is nodding and laughing at me, and then he turns saying:

“Look, you have to remember that there’s always good and bad people in every race and nation. Remember also the reason why we all are on this trip, not only for the stolen children but also for your daughter . . .”

Jollya takes me aside in private, saying:

“His name is Tavon.” And she taps on my arm, encouraging me to speak to him.

“Eh, Tavon, look man, would you accept my apology?”

He signs immediately with his hand that it’s okay; it was really awkward to make that joke . . .

“Wouldn’t it be easier if we rode a car instead of walking, struggling with every step we take?” I say, trying to change the subject.

“We would be caught by your Explorers if we did so, and anyway we are close enough.” Finley is pointing at the massive barrier of Nopoly, which is clear and near

III Inside Nopoly, Again

16- The Bloody Path

We are approaching a dilapidated construction surrounded by fallen trees.

"Why do we stop here?" I ask.

"Under this debris is our way to enter Nopoly," Finley answers me; and he turns to the rest, saying: "Come on guys, let's remove all this rubble here!" He points to a specific area in the place.

Everyone is starting to dislodge the broken pieces of the building. I notice that there is a broken doll on the corner; this building was probably a school, a hospital, or a toy store, I guess . . .

"Good job team," says Finley while opening a metal drain cover.

"Don't you have any other way to manage your plan other than the sewers?" I ask ironically.

"Unfortunately not, because the government can't see that deep . . ." Finley replies.

"Or maybe they don't like to play on the slide," I comment, pointing at the stinky slope that shows up under the cover.

"Well, after you Mr. Harley!"

"I've never been scared to take the first step, Mr. Finley," I say, sliding down to a dark sewer.

While the others are sliding down, I'm checking the place with my spotlight.

"Now, follow me guys!" the boss says.

We get into a little tighter place, and there, I can feel myself treading on the water, which has a dark red color. Before I ask about the reason for this color, we end up at a rusted door that leads us to a very creepy place. And it gets even creepier when we are going down the stairs. The place is full of blood; it's literally a pool of blood coming up to our knees.

"Where did all this blood come from?" I ask, disgusted.

"Nopoly," a young man answers immediately.

"The place wasn't this messy first time we discovered it," he continues.

"Yeah, I agree with you, Ben," says Tavon.

"Have you been in the city before and just escaped?"

"No, but Tavon and I were sewer workers, and we had a look at the sewer plans for this neighborhood, so we helped the Free Ones find a way to the drain of Nopoly," Ben answers me.

"Then we discovered this dump, which shows how broken our humanity is," Tavon replies.

While our legs are swimming in this dark red blood, a lady screams:

"Jesus Christ!"

"What is it, Sena? Oh my god! Is this a dead body?!" Jollya freaks out.

"Come and see. There are many of them floating everywhere here!" a guy says with dread.

"Where are all these bodies coming from?" Metallic sounds stop me from talking; and when we direct our lights at the sound source, they show a terrible thing.

"Ask no more Harley, look at the dead people sliding from these gates!" Finley says, pointing at similar gates around the area.

"What the hell! More dead people are sliding into here . . ."

"That explains why I didn't see any graveyard in the city, nor on the map that VI showed us . . ." Jollya says with so much sadness in her quiet voice.

"So is that . . ."

"Most of these people were victims of human experiments, who probably appeared as demons to the Nopolyens . . ." Jollya carries on in pain.

"Human experiments?" I'm questioning.

"Yes . . . They're using people from outside who are the rare cases because, basically, they don't have to be in Nopoly; just like the African man who has been taken to the city even though he wasn't in any racist group. They take some of these rare cases to do experiments on them; and when these cases fail to give good results, they end up with a crazy person—"

"Or a damn demon, right?" Finley interrupts Jollya.

"But the others, who are trying to get into the city 'illegally,' according to Nopoly's law, just become crazy with the help of the scientists there . . ." Jollya continues, clarifying, leaving me with so much astonishment that I share with the rest of the group.

While I'm considering Jollya's words and feeling the floating bodies touching my legs, I assume that at least one of these bodies belongs to the victims I killed in the city.

Deeper we go, and more bodies are gathering in a very creepy way until we end up at a catacomb when we turn right. The first thing we notice is the increase in the insects' number in the place.

Suddenly, Finley grabs a wrench from his bag, opens a specific gate, and starts to punch the metal from inside with the wrench.

"Are you calling more dead to be invited here?"

"Good one, Harley," Finley replies, and then he shouts: "Come on Eugene!"

"What is happening now?"

"Eugene is one of the Free Ones who are living inside secretly; he will help us to get inside Nopoly," Jollya answers me.

"Did I meet any of Them in there, except my lovely wife?"

"Actually, yeah! Cason Baker; do you remember him?"

"I think that I've heard this name before. Is it the guy who wanted to go out of the city, and I recommended that he go to Dr. Diana?"

"The very same; and thanks to his hug, I could track you down in the city by a very small tracker he implanted underneath your skin," Jollya replies.

"What a plan!" I say in astonishment and continue, "I hope he is fine . . ."

"I don't think so, especially after his meeting with Dr. Diana," Jollya suggests.

"Why didn't your people, who were already in, save all the children before I got out of the city?" I direct my question to

Finley who is still punching the gate. He stops punching and turns to me, answering:

"For Jollya, you and Lori were the main mission, but for me, I needed a mask from a person who works with the government, and this is how my interest and Jollya's intersected; so, you were the common factor." And he continues making noise with the wrench.

Jollya comes to me touching my arm, telling me:

"Everything will be good as long as we are together." I hold her hands, confirming that too and responding: "forever . . ."

Finley stops his annoying noise when something that sounds heavy seems to come from the same gate.

"Let's climb to . . . Nopoly!" Finley says in excitement while holding the chain that has dropped.

"Another slide?! How can we climb it?" I question him.

"You have to use three things. Your hands to hold the chain, your legs to support your hand and help you to move on, and your brain to always think of a solution," Finley replies before disappearing into the darkness of the gate.

The place feels so tight because it's dark and full of blood.

"So, this is how your men got into Nopoly," I say, struggling with every word because of the climbing exercise.

"Yes Harley, and no one noticed, nor the police captain, hahaha."

"Now I'm sure you are the real Satan, Finley . . ." I respond and he keeps laughing.

The nightmare ends when I get out of that endless grave. But I find myself surrounded by hanging dead bodies.

"Is this a human butcher's?!"

"You said it. Now, Harley, you need to be quiet and no more questions until we get out of this place, but you can use your lowest tone," Finley whispers.

A man is coming to us while we are hiding using the hanging bodies, and he says when he approaches us:

"Follow me in silence!"

I believe that is Eugene who Finley was calling down there in his primitive way.

After a short walk among the dead, we get into the workers' washroom, and we stop beside a bunch of hanging VI-masked people.

"Each of you has to put the mask on directly after taking it off from them, and then put their suit on you; hurry up and choose your mask . . ." Eugene says while locking the door; and here I jump, irritated:

"I'll never put that thing on my face again. Are you guys crazy?"

"Don't be silly. These masks are modified. We are not that silly to use them as the government of Nopoly wants," Tavon says and Jollya nods yes, so that is enough encouragement for me.

I've never thought about being the creature who is taking someone's face, because in my last life in the city, that was considered as an act for the demons. And here I am; I'm the demon in Nopolyens' eyes now. I'm the enemy they have to kill. What an irony!

I take off the gas mask and the radioactive suit after a quick wash and clean. And I put that creepy mask on my face. The sharp wires don't hurt me like the idea of living someone's else life with all the ideology that person has.

Now, I'm officially a Nopolyen citizen who is ready to go through the fake life again, but with real knowledge.

"We'll separate into two groups; Chris, Tavon, Sena, Ben, and Steven in one group and the rest with me. Our mission is to find where the newly taken children are," the boss is planning, but I get a little confused by the new faces of us.

"But wait! Where are Tavon, Chris, and Sami?" I ask.

"Because we are in Nopoly, there is no place for colored skin here, but you can see them if you turn the mask off," Tavon says, showing me a very small button on the side of the mask.

"Thank you, and I would say that I prefer your real faces guys . . ."

"I'd say the same. Good luck with finding Lori," responds a nice brown man, and I'm nodding thanks to him without even remembering his name.

17. Layers of Pain, End to the Brain

Now, the five of us are in the beautiful city that is dancing with people's happiness, but things get change when I switch the Virtual Illusion off; the real face of Nopoly is revealed. The whole city is built from the same cold iron, and the huge barrier isn't only for protection; it contains many massive divided screens that simulate the sky, sunlight, and probably the stars in the night. What I saw in the VI was totally different from what I see now. The trees are nothing but wide electricity poles with something like sprays at the top of them; the demons in circuses are poorly colored human beings, and the horses are creatures that nearly look like humans but with longer arms and more muscles. They are human, actually; there is no doubt about it. I feel so bad and ashamed of myself for living in such a city like Nopoly that I can make no comment, especially when I remember Ario and how I owned him; I owned a human that seemed to be just a horse to me, and I treated him like an animal!

What torments me is seeing abnormal people seem crazy—rare cases, according to what Jollya said—and get shot by the police in front of pedestrians who look so frightened. The whole atmosphere here is horrible and inhuman!

"Why didn't I have the ability to see the real world as I do now when I was here before?" I ask.

"I think there are a couple of people who have this ability, unlike the others; from my experience, people like ExA, some doctors, nurses, and those who know about the Bezman project have this ability, and they keep their memories," Jollya answers me in a very low voice.

"And workers like us," Alexa adds sarcastically.

"But it seems that the government will not like us," Finley says, looking at the police, who are hovering around the area.

"I think, we have to hide for a while," I speculate.

"We don't have enough time. First of all, we need to find the latest taken children; second, we'll collect all children, including Lori; and third, we have to take them out of here safely," Finley responds.

"So, where do we have to start?"

"The hidden places that we discovered in your VI mask . . ."

"What hidden places do you mean?"

"You were a captain in the police force, but you were betrayed by the VI with no recognition for the reality, so that's why it wasn't possible to you to know the whole plan of the city."

"Do you mean that we need to check all the hidden places?" I press.

"Or we can borrow a very important person's mask, and then we'll have the whole plan. Luckily, your mask, Harley, has names for very important people with their locations," Finley suggests.

"Sorry to bother you, but I need to check your identity by my crow, ladies and gentlemen," a police officer says as he jumps out of nowhere.

"Of course, officer," says Finley, smiling and stretches his hand happily in the air, and the crow, which is actually a flying camera, drops down immediately.

"Oh, the crow has fallen; is it OK, sir?" Finley asks innocently.

"It's OK; it happens. Can I see your IDs instead?"

"Of course! Here." Finley hands it to the officer, and we all do the same.

"Have a nice day, Mr. Billy." The police officer salutes us.

"Thank you, officer. You too," Finley responds, as calm as a toad in the sun.

"What an actor, Mr. Billy! You are multitalented," I utter sarcastically, showing that I am impressed.

"To survive, you'll have to follow the flow, but not drown in it," he responds confidently.

"Nice speech, but what did you do to that 'crow'?"

"I threw some of my Super-Nano magic from a thrower in my wrist." Finley shows me the fake classic watch on his arm.

"So, every single one of you has something to throw, except me!"

"No, Harley, you have your mouth, which can throw tons of questions," Finley says, laughing.

"Haha! Personally, I think we all have abilities, but you may haven't discovered them yet," Sami comments kindly, and Jollya agrees.

While we are walking in the city, pretending that we are just five normal citizens, when in reality, we're planning how to acquire a very important person's mask, Sami asks me:

"Can you remember the most important character you've met here?"

"The Commandos, some scientists, and a doctor."

"Is it Dr. Diana, whose face I used to get you out?" Jollya is asking.

"Yeah . . . yeah, it was the one who wanted to play with my memory—or, probably, with my life. She is a horrible person."

"I've got an idea. Jollya, do you remember what the real face of Diana looked like?" Finley asks after a short consideration.

"Yes, I do." As she starts describing her, slowly, we realize that we have a lady who nearly has Diana's appearance.

"Alexa, you'll be the new Diana!" Finley says excitedly.

"How?" she asks.

Finley takes us to a corner of the fake park and says, "You will go to the doctor because you have mental problems because of your job. When she moves toward you, press this little button in your palm, and you'll use your nano thrower to jam the camera in Diana's clinic."

"How long will it be jammed?"

"A half minute, so remember to take her face and suit as fast as possible; and don't forget to make sure that the real Diana will stay asleep in a comfortable place," Finley says. "OK?"

"Like the wardrobe that I used to hide her before," Jollya says, smiling.

"Is it possible to trick her again in the same way?" I wonder aloud.

"She didn't realize anything because I put her face back and left her sitting in her office before she woke up; she probably thought that she had just a little nap."

"And what about the camera?"

"I used the same technique that Alexa will use: the Nano Ants."

"And what next?" Alexa is asking.

"You will become Dr. Diana, who wants to date a professor. Oh, yeah, Professor James Wallgang, who will accept, right, Alexa?"

"Don't worry, I have my ways; but what then?"

"A romantic night and some fun with a young lady like Diana; will the old man think about—"

"Why would I do that?"

Finley starts walking, nodding to us with his head to move on, and he continues, "You don't need to do anything; just let him be himself. When you meet him in his place, get him drunk, and put him to sleep with these sleeping needles. After that, take all the information from Wallgang's mask to this little computer, and leave him sleeping in peace; leave him as Diana, and you'll find us waiting for you in this place."

"This place looks familiar," I comment.

"It's right in front of Dr. Diana's place. Now, Alexa, go in and do exactly what I told you. When you go out, give us a sign that it is you—twirl around like a little princess, and we will watch for you from the next block, over there. Carry on with the mission, and when you're done with it, come to the park we were in, and don't forget the princess dance."

"Haha, you're just crazy . . . But it's an epic plan; I'll do it. Wish me luck, guys."

"No wishing; you have to do it because the whole mission is counting on your reactions and your intelligence now, and I know you'll never disappoint me." Finley stops talking, and Alexa signs yes before leaving us.

A half hour passes, and Alexa doesn't appear, neither with the mask nor without it; and our anxiety starts to rise.

"Shall I go in to see what happened to Alexa?" Sami suggests.

"Patience, brother; she may decide to go out at the end of the work day."

"Are you kidding? Do we have to stay here for hours waiting for her?" I ask Finley nervously. "I will go to find my daughter by myself . . ." I continue, but Finley grabs my hand saying:

"Your daughter can't be found impulsively; you can't even the map of this city, so hold on, my friend."

"Exactly. Besides, I've searched for Lori all over the city, but I couldn't find her anywhere. So please, just calm down and we will definitely find her. And keep in mind that the time in Nopoly is different; twelve hours is one day here, so let's give Alexa one more half-hour," Jollya convinces me.

"What a place! Why do they cut the day in half?" asks Tavon.

"They haven't cut it; they've sped up the time. And I have no idea why they're doing that," Jollya answers.

After a couple of minutes, a flying camera comes to Diana's clinic, and after a minute, it flies away.

"What can be happening there?" I ask Finley.

"Good things, I hope!"

Finley's hope is confirmed when the doctor, who terrified me, appears, but I feel so much better now after seeing a princess twirl.

I'm trying to ignore all the crazy things that happened in the city and just look around to maybe see Lori by some chance; even though the children have masks on their little faces, which scares me the most, I know I can recognize my daughter from her beautiful light brown hair and sweet smile. I also keep an eye on Alexa, whom we are following at a distance.

When the light of the artificial sun goes down, Alexa approaches a huge building, and we stop following. The place Alexa has entered is full of soldiers—so many soldiers for a single professor!

I ask Finley about this man, but he offers no response. He seems so nervous, waiting for Alexa's return, that I decide to reduce my curiosity for a bit.

"He does that when he is super nervous," Jollya tells me while holding my hand.

"Excuse me! Are you guys fine?" An officer comes asking.

"Oh! Yes . . . yes, officer. I'm just not sure which restaurant we shall test: Kenturcky or MacDonat," Finley says calmly.

"Well, MacDonat is my favorite, especially the burger bread, which is donut bread. Try it out, and move on from here, please!"

"Thank you, officer," we all say and follow Finley.

"How can we see Alexa from here?"

"Harley . . . Harley! I like your questions, but let us act as normal as possible until the officer's attention moves away from us. Let's see, hmmm, I'd take a beef burger; and you guys?"

"Are you serious Finley? Is it time to eat?" Jollya growls in a very low tone.

"Trust me, sis . . ."

"I do, but I'll not eat anything; I don't want you to test this food either," Jollya says, and then she breathes in and out before ordering: "Chicken burger."

"That's just crazy," I say, trying to remind him of our main issue: the kids.

"I'll choose for you, my friend; hmmm, Happy Don. What about you, Sami?"

"French fries, please," he responds to that crazy Finley.

I look around us at the happy customers, who are eating their meals impatiently.

When the meals are served, I look at the meal, which seems to be the only thing normal in this city, but Finley interrupts my thinking, saying: "Get the meat and chicken out of your burgers and put it in this plastic bag—now!" We do what he asks. After that, he says, "Keep an eye on the sky, and if you notice a flying camera going to where we left Alexa, leave everything and start moving toward the building, and I will follow you."

"Where are you going now?" I ask.

"I'm going to the bathroom, Harley. Do you want to help me? Then come with me."

"No thanks. Bon appetit," I reply before he leaves, giving me a weird smile.

"What a disgusting man!" I express my feeling about him with my face.

"At least he didn't take the donuts," Sami says while stuffing fries in his mouth.

Jollya is not eating; she is watching the sky as Finley asked.

A short period later, Finley comes back and sits in his chair in silence.

"What happened back there? Does it stink that bad in this restaurant's toilet?" I try to make fun of this crazy Finley.

"Harley, stop!" Jollya says emotionally and she is about to cry.

Finley didn't raise his head when he first came back, but he starts talking now, saying:

"The meat . . . it is made . . . from . . . human flesh."

"What?" all of us scream, but my voice is full of anger, ignoring the customers who are looking at us.

"I was examining the meat to see if my concerns are correct, and they are."

"This is unacceptable—inhumanity!" I react with rising anger.

"I . . . I'm sorry. I didn't want to—"

"Taking a kid from a mommy, making food from the human body, turning poor people to a property . . . this is our broken humanity," Sami interrupts Jollya, his broken voice full of sadness.

"Let us go out . . ." Finley says with a quiet voice.

I'm so shocked that I cannot move with the rest, who get up to leave the table. My hands are trembling, and my legs can't hold me up.

"Let's go out of this place, Harley; come on, honey," Jollya says. She supports me from the left and Sami from the right because the shock is paralyzing my brain.

A voice asks, "Is he okay?"

"Yes, officer. He's just drunk, hehehe," Finley answers her.

"Hahaha, have a good night then!"

After the officer moves away, and we wait for Alexa from a distance, I collapse in tears.

Jollya comes closer to me saying:

"Oh, baby, baby, what's the matter?"

"I am a monster, a horrible person who deserves to die . . ." and I continue crying.

"Harley! Don't say that, honey."

"I ate human flesh! What a horrible person I am . . . I am a freaking cannibal!" I shout, crying for what I did. I am the real monster, and all of these damn Nopolyens are, too!

"Have you eaten Lori's meat?" I attack a pedestrian while screaming at him hysterically. I hear nothing but noises in my head; and the blood feels like it's rising to my eyes, which will explode any second. I am unaware of my surroundings until I find myself seized by the police.

In the prison, I regain my senses and realize that I'm not the only prisoner. Jollya and Finley have joined me.

"Welcome back to the city you belong to, Mr. John Cooper—former police captain and traitor to Nopoly now," Some one who look a doctor says.

"Who the hell are you?" I ask.

"Dr. Stephen Harris. You surely remember me," he says removing his Recognition Face and laughing a scary, confident laugh.

"I'm the one involved, so leave the others alone, and I'll tell you everything you want!"

"Harley!" shouts Jollya in astonishment.

"Leave him; he has lost his mind anyway," Finley responds hopelessly.

I'm considering how crazy I was when I ruined the whole plan because of my recklessness. But, regardless, I'll never find Lori. She is gone forever, and so am I.

Dr. Harris leaves the prison, ignoring my proposal, which was a hopeless attempt to get out of here with the others. Finley, from behind the bars that separate us in the cage, says, looking at Jollya, "It was my fault to bring him with us here, but it's your fault also."

"I'm . . . sorry," I say in a low voice.

"What did you say? Sorry? You don't have anything other than saying *sorry*?"

"No, Finley . . . there is probably hope that someone will save us, just like what happened to me when Jollya—"

"There is no one! I was the head for that unpleasant mission of getting you out, but now there is no one who knows what happened to us. Alexa will be just caught, Sami has probably been shot, and the whole plan is wrecked thanks to you!" Finley interrupts me emotionally.

"How can you be the head of the mission when Jollya followed me and came in with the army without any contact with you?"

"Oh my God! Here we go again with the stupid questions!"

"Finley!" Jollya signals to him to calm down and continues, "I didn't meet Finley, but I was meeting Martin, whom I entered the city with, in a place we set up together, and he was the connection between me and Finley after a couple of efforts to take you out of the city." She adds, "I do agree with Harley that we should not lose hope. I believe that God will save us somehow."

"Sure," Finley responds to Jollya. But Jollya doesn't believe in God, as I know! Maybe she said that to soften the atmosphere and calm Finley down.

An hour later, Dr. Stephen comes back with his creepy tools, saying:

"Two sneaky demons used our VI mask and a traitorous captain; did you enjoy the experience? Oh, I like the amendments you added to the mask; and because of removing the voice recorder that you had on your masks, you'll have to tell me everything about yourselves." He stops talking but never stops looking at each one of us like a psychopath. "Otherwise, I have some tools to help you talk. Bring them to the blue room," the crazy doctor orders, and six soldiers come to take us.

I try to escape from the soldiers, but the chains are fastened around my arms, my feet, and my neck. I don't want to escape for myself, but I want to end Jollya's struggle and release her at least. Finley is looking at me angrily, but Jollya is checking the place which looks so creepy. And we end up sitting on chairs, bound and helpless.

"I'll start with you, Mr. Cooper."

As soon as the doctor says that name, I remember the pain I felt the day I was seized like it was yesterday. I feel the fear running in my blood, which is flooding my body so fast because of my racing heart. There is no way I will be saved; who I was deceiving when I thought that someone will save us? We are done . . .

"Dr. Stephen, I'll tell you everything you need."

"Perfect. I'll hook up the lie detector and start recording, though."

"One condition. I want you to release the lady."

"Harley! No!"

"Oh, are you in love with her? I see what is happening now. I have a better idea. What if I persuade you to talk in my way in front of your lovely lady, huh?" he says while choosing what tool he'll use to torture me; he decides on the drill machine.

"No, no, no. Stop! What are you doing?" I scream dreadfully, ignoring the others' screams and shouts and focusing on the noise of the drill.

An assistance starts to put some kind of helmet on my head, and the doctor starts to put things on the helmet, saying:

"Love is a beautiful feeling. The lover can do anything to the pair—literally anything. I used to be in love with a man, but we had part because of the war, and I forced myself to change the idea of being interested in men. You know . . . according to the law in Nopoly, every couple must be a man and woman to compensate for the human losses and to revive our nation again."

"Where is your fragile freedom? Why don't you revolt against Nopoly's government then?" Finley asks the doctor, who is putting on the helmet on Sami's head.

"Nice try to get some extra minutes with your memory. The reason for the fabricated crises between different religions and different nations: was to create emotional and intellectual differences, ignite endless wars, global epidemics, spread the hate, support the concept of nationalities, and promote ideas that persuade people not to create steady families and just living life for fun. These were invisible tools to control the birth rate and save the economy, according to the book *The Secret of the Selection*."

After he's finished putting the helmets on our heads, he turns to me again, saying: "To be gay is considered a part of the fun, but I've changed my thoughts and feelings only for my nation. Are you ready to be changed as well by telling everything to me?"

He comes to me, looks directly into my eyes, and asks, "How did you get into the city? How many of you are still in here? What is your intention for getting back with those freaks?"

When he gets no answer from me, he hides his smile with the mask, and the drill starts working again; but this time it's so close to my head.

The pain that I get from the metal on my head is unbearable. When the drill touches my skull, a horrible headache, like I've never had before, brings a red haze to my vision and hits me with such disorienting dizziness that I involuntarily scream like a madman. No voice is audible to me, including my own screams; I only hear the creaking sound in my skull. I feel the blinding pain reaching my brain, and I close my eyes, screaming even louder.

The drilling has stopped, but the pain is not; in fact, it has increased. I can't think of anything but how to end this feeling and avoid this suffering.

"Waaa . . . aaaaah . . . I . . . ah . . ." That's all I can say to express my feelings. I have no clue what is going on, because I can't see properly, but I see no blue light anymore. All I see is dark spots in my vision; I have been blinded perhaps!

"Dr. Diana!" I hear someone saying when the door is suddenly flung open.

"Let me continue this work, Dr. Stephen." And two shots ring out across the room. I'm still hearing the ringing I got after the drilling, and I feel extreme pain.

"Oh my God! Look what they did to you," someone says and unties me. I think it's Jollya. But I do feel something still on my head.

They are talking, but I don't care about the subject; I only need to get rid of this terrible pain.

Jollya puts something in my mouth and gives me a cup of water.

"Everything will be fine, honey, trust me," Jollya says through tears, but I can't respond to her or tell her to stop crying.

As soon as the helmet has been removed from my head, the blood runs down my face, and I can taste it in my mouth. What I understand from the conversation is that Alexa got all the information; and the most important information she mentions is that all the children are safe, and they should not be killed under any circumstances because they are the treasure of Nopoly.

"They are coming any minute," Alexa exclaims.

"I'll heal him as fast as possible," Jollya responds and looks at me, whispering, "It's a small wound, so don't worry, baby." I nod yes even though she's not telling the truth; I know that she's saying it to calm me, and she starts cleaning the wound to bandage it.

"No, no. It hurts! I only need some water. We have to continue the mission," I say slowly, drawing on all the little power I have.

"OK, OK. Hold on." Jollya is trying to stop me from moving to wrap the bandage around my head.

"Who is coming?" I whisper to Jollya.

"Soldiers!" someone shouts before Jollya opens her mouth.

The crossfire starts, and it's so painful to hear, but my smart wife has realized that and puts earplugs into my ears.

The pain begins to ease, and my vision is clearer, so I decide to join my team and not give up because there is still hope to find my daughter, Lori. And my lovely wife is supporting me as I overcome my dizziness and stand properly.

After a while, the shooting has stopped. It seems that we defeated them, even though I didn't do anything, and we start moving.

"Alexa, where is our stuff?" Finley is asking.

"Wait a minute; it's in room S30," she answers as she busies herself with her computer, which is connecting with our VI masks she's holding.

"Now, you can use the VI safely."

"What do you mean, safely? And why would we need them now?" I question Alexa.

"As you know, these masks had been modified, and I've sent all the information I got from professor James's masks to yours."

"Nice work, thank you."

"You have to thank Sami also, who informed me what happened to you because of your rage."

"Thank you, brother." I direct my speech to Sami, and he gives me a smile. I've never used this word before, but I feel that the person who saved us from a painful death deserves my brotherhood.

After taking our things and donning our VI masks, Finley says confidently, "Our next destination is Future Kid Lab."

18. Unexpected Things

On our way to the lab, we find that the army has spread out in the city, and they are striking us from all directions. The electricity is cut off in the city, and the Nopolyens and the police are acting so strangely; they all seem blind!

"Finn! What are you throwing, man? Your bombs aren't working!"

"They aren't . . ." he stops because he's busy shooting. "Use your pierced brain! This thing is an emulator hologram; look what it can do," Finley says, scanning me with it; then he throws it after timing it.

"Look how it projects you there. This is how we are misdirecting the enemy," he clarifies while shooting.

It's such crazy and intelligent technology, especially seeing how my 3D image is moving, holding the weapon, looking like a normal person!

Suddenly, we hear several rockets launching all around the city.

"What now?" I exclaim, freaking out.

"Something unreassuring," Finley answers.

After a while, several explosions have shocked the whole city, which gives us the opportunity to leave the soldiers behind. Gold-colored clouds start rising everywhere in the atmosphere, and warning sirens sound and announce orders to stay home because Nopoly is under demons' attacks, and that everyone will be blind for a while, but they don't need to worry; however, everyone outside will be in danger of being killed by demons!

"What in the hell is that?

"Harley, no time for questions. Everyone put the gas mask on, and let's hurry to save the kids!"

The people in the streets, are getting crazier with every passing second; they look so scary and act like zombies, and sharp appendages have been grown on their hands.

"I do believe in zombies now!" I shout.

"I've read about a chemical drug that turns people into creatures that act mindlessly and violently," Jollya says.

"Guys, just run! We don't need to kill them!" Finley orders, and we stop shooting.

"Why does the government need to do that with its folk?" I ask.

"Alexa! Watch out!" Sami shouts at the same time as Jollya starts screaming dreadfully.

"Alexa! Nooo!"

Two of these crazy people catch Alexa and start to shred her body with their hands, which are full of sharp appendages.

The bullets don't save Alexa, but they do tell her that we'll fight to the last breath.

Sami is calling out to her that we'll never forget her, but I bet she hasn't been able to hear anything for a while.

"Changing the plan; anyone or anything gets close to us, finish it!" Finley utters determinedly.

"They are using their citizens against us in all possible ways!" Jollya says with anger and pain in her voice.

The situation is getting crazier and more dangerous with all these trans-humans; they have become the real demons here! Their heads are moving from side to side at a very fast speed, and they are stretching their hands to shred the next victim.

I'm running while burning on the inside to find Lori in all this chaos, and I find myself standing on a dead-end street.

“What? It’s blocked!” Sami says.

“Maybe there is a hidden door or something,” Jollya suggests.

“How do we know that all the information that Alexa got from the professor is accurate?” I ask nervously.

“Why do you think the Nopolyens are acting like blind?” Sami asks me back waiting for me to answer.

“They were blind from reality the whole time.” Finley replies looking at the ground, and then he looks at me saying:

“I told Alexa to shoot the flare gun after finishing the mission; that would signal the Free Ones, who are hiding in the city, to launch the Super-Nano Ants.” Finley shocks me with his answer. The little changers have been used again!

“So, you did it again, and because of you, the whole city is getting crazy . . . And Alexa is dead because of that! Don’t you care?”

“Harley, I’m really glad to find you caring about the others, but you should know that Nopoly has launched the chemical; it deceived everyone, and it’s been doing a lot of inhuman things until this moment; so, please calm down and think of your daughter.”

“Honey, their actions led them to be in this environment, and these are the consequences,” Jollya says.

While we are confused and looking for the hidden door, a sound from behind us gets closer and closer.

“Behind the carriage!” Finley shouts.

As soon as we get behind the parked carriage, three trucks pull onto the street. The ground starts shaking, and it feels like we are moving down slowly.

“Do you feel this? Or is it only me?” asks Jollya.

“No, Jollya. The ground . . . is moving. It seems that we are in a huge elevator!” I respond.

As we descend below ground level, the earth closes over us and the lights turn on in the elevator while we are slowly lowered with the trucks. I assume that we are going to a hidden place. and this place is the laboratory we are searching for.

We stop moving, and many soldiers with gas masks on their faces get out of the trucks.

"Let's go, guys, quietly," Finley whispers.

We follow the soldiers from a distance to see where they'll end up—before we end them. The soldiers stop to open a metal door; twelve of them are there, but Jollya has only five hypnotic needles.

"It's time to kill nice and clean," Finley says while attaching the silencer to his gun.

The unfortunate twelve become eight, but they do realize that in a second. Sami is using the hologram thing to rush the five, who think we are throwing a bomb, and they become only three.

They are struggling to survive by shooting everywhere, but I don't think they have a chance. We come to the last soldier, who surrenders and begs us, "Please! I'll do anything you want!"

"Well, I'll think of that if you are advantageous to us," Finley says calmly.

"Take off your mask!" Sami orders her.

"Where is Lori? Where is she?!" I grasp her jacket aggressively

"Harley!" Jollya stops me with a look, telling me to be wise, and she adds, "The kids are in there, right?"

"Yes."

"Look, if you want to survive, you have to work with us, and to work with us, you have to prove your loyalty." Finley has been discussing with her until now, and I don't know why!

"I have no other options, but I guarantee you that I'm loyal."

"I can't fully trust you, so I'll have to do this," Finley utters, raising a pistol toward the soldier. He shoots her in the neck, ignoring her pleas and Jollya's disapproval, but she doesn't die!

"I'm alive! Your bullet didn't work on me!"

"Oh, immortal soldier! Are you the real superwoman?" Finley seems scared as he picks up an apple from his pocket. "Don't brag, because I have this apple and Another Chance pistol," this madman continues.

"Finley, have you lost your mind?" As soon as I say that, Finley shoots the apple and then throws it in the air. The apple was in a perfect state, before that crazy man pressed a button in the pistol, and the apple explodes immediately in the air.

"So, you have one more chance to live, Miss . . .?"

"Lisa," she answers, shocked and terrified.

"Well, Miss Lisa, you'll be at my service, and if you prove yourself a faithful soldier to us, I'll take the little bullet out of your neck, and you'll live peacefully. Give me your hand if you are in!" And she gives him her hand to stand up and starts to move with us.

"So, what do you want from the lab?"

"The children, whom your government has taken, have to get back to their families. Don't you agree, Lisa?" I say.

"I do understand your feelings but they'll not let you out with the children," she says.

"Don't worry. Everything goes well with a good plan," Finley responds.

We find ourselves at another metal door that is locked with an eye scanner lock.

"I'm glad that I developed my ants to attack certain things only." Finley seems happy and satisfied. "Open the door for us, please!" he continues.

While the soldier is scanning her eye, Sami asks her, "What would happen if we open this door by force?"

"You'll be hit with many bullets because there are automatic machine guns on the other side, which can be active in case of a break-in."

I can see the stress on Sami's face, so I put my hand on his shoulder and give him an encouraging nod to let him know that everything is OK.

"Why would you join them?" he asks her.

"Humanitarian reasons. The terrorists outside are waiting for the opportunity to kill the rest of Americans, and they're wanting to take our loot and take over the last living place on Earth, probably. And the reason for taking the kids to the city is to save them from being eaten by their starving, violent parents or by these terrorists out there; these are the reasons the government gives us."

"False pretenses! This is not right at all! I was a citizen of Nopoly before I got out of the city with a little help . . ." And I look at Jollya smiling. "And then I lived with the people whom this government considers terrorists, demons, outsiders, and so on. But I swear I've seen the best example of humanity with them. These outcasts from the government not only saved my life and my wife's life, but they are also here to save the kidnapped children, including my daughter . . . Lori."

Jollya gives me a hug from the side, supporting her broken man who has shed a tear, and I can see Samir's glittery eyes smiling, telling me that he's proud of me.

The soldier stops working like she's considering what I've said, and then she says, "I've lived in this protected city, and I couldn't know that; so what other choices did I have?"

The door is opening, and my heart is jumping with happiness. I leave the group, running to see my lovely little daughter, but I stop when I see many rooms down the stairs and the nurses looking at me in surprise.

"Who are you? And how did you get in here?"

"It's doesn't matter. Where is Lori Woodman? Where is my daughter?" And I feel a hand from behind, cautioning me to calm down.

"Sorry, ladies, but this man is insistent," Finley says.

We get down to the shocked nurses, and I begin searching for Lori among all the kids who are in their glass-walled rooms.

"Where is she?" I shout, and I start going into room after room, searching among the white-dressed kids for my little Lori.

The surgery rooms are full of children, whose blood are on the doctor's hands. Other kids have little VI masks on their faces!

"This is madness! What are you doing with these kids?" I ask the doctors in a trembling voice. The nurses are pushing me and shouting at me to leave, telling that these children are meant to live in Nopoly, and their real parents are Nopolyens.

"What Nopolyens? I'm her father!"

"Biologically!" one of them says.

"On papers, you can see clearly that the kids who are living in Nopoly belong to Nopoly!" another one is claiming.

"This is ridiculous!" I say as I raise my gun to one of the nurses' head. The kids start to cry and scream, but a voice interrupts all these sounds.

"Freeze, don't move!" It is Lisa holding a gun on Jollya.

"Drop the guns, all of you. Now!"

"Please don't do it!" I beg the soldier, dropping my gun, and the others do the same.

As soon as our guns have been confiscated, we are seized by the kind nurses.

We are sitting on our knees, and that Lisa is asking if Lori is okay. The head nurse gives no answer, but signs to the soldier to follow her somewhere.

"That was very clever to let her alive. What were you thinking?" I say. Finley seems frustrated and doesn't answer me.

"Don't you have the heart to feel? We are parents, just like all the others who only want to live with their children. Isn't our simple, humble right?"

"Jollya, don't bother with them; they're either deceived or they have accepted to work here, so they know everything already, and they won't care," Finley says, giving up, or maybe he's pretending to . . .

"We do care. We saved many children from extinction because of the harmful life out of the city!"

"This city has been built with so much hate, racism, and fakeness; it's not the right place to raise the kids," Jollya responds, looking at a little child who is looking back at her with an innocent smile.

I stop listening to these heartless people and start thinking about how can we can escape. There is no way to give up now.

While I'm trying to free my arm, that treacherous soldier comes with the head nurse.

"Harl, you asked why do I trust Lisa, and the answer is: I thought she had some humanity left in her heart," says Finley.

"Thanks for the late answer, Finn!" I respond, right before Lisa squats to talk to me, ignoring what Finley said.

She asks, "What's your surname?"

"It's not your damn business!" I shut this heartless soldier down, and she is silent.

Jollya interjects, "It's Woodman. Why are you asking?"

"Jollya! Why?"

"I thought you were looking for your daughter, but since you aren't answering, it means that you don't care about her anymore," Lisa says standing up again.

"My name is Harley Woodman and my daughter is Lori Woodman. Do you know where is she? Please!" My eyes are full of warm tears, and Jollya's are also.

"I know where is she," Lisa utters while she's untying me and the others, ignoring what the head nurse is babbling.

"She's in the first building in the city, which has a statue for Dinis," she says, showing us a picture of the statue. I am astonished for a couple of minutes.

"Thank you so much," Jollya says, grasping Lisa's hand, which surprises the soldier.

"Why would you help us?" I ask her.

"Because he thought I may have some humanity left," Lisa answers, pointing at Finley, and she continues, "These folders can help you to understand things better."

"You are really treacherous! These are super-secret information! Why would you do that? You will regret it, I promise!" the head nurse shouts like a crazy person.

"I did regret becoming a part of all of this. Now you, Harley, go and find Lori before things will get worse. Anything else I can help with?"

"Actually, yes. Can you and Sami get the kids in this lab to the trucks and take them out of this damned city?" Finley asks Lisa.

"But there are so many. The children and babies!" Sami says.

Finley places his Chance gun against Lisa's neck, and he says, "I've removed it, so don't worry."

"I'm in," Lisa responds nodding yes; and Finley smiles at her before he turns to Sami and throws the gun to him.

"You can use it on the head nurse. She will cooperate with you when she realizes what this can do to her head; and use all the bullets to gain many loyal ones. Now, Lisa is one of us, and I do trust her just like you, my friends, so keep that in mind, Sami.

"On our way out, I'll use the flare gun to call all the Free Rebels to help you get the kids out. If, for any reason, Nopoly's exit gates are locked, use the Nano Explosives!" Sami nods yes.

"Are you coming with us?" I direct the question to Finley.

"You'll get lost without me. Now let's go guys—and thank you, Lisa," Finley finishes before we leave the laboratory.

We get out of the lab with so much energy because Finley's goal has almost been reached. The only thing left now is finding my little beautiful angel and taking her out of here safely.

19. Fighting the Terrorists

At a fast walk, we get out of the lab, wary of any kind of danger we may face in a city that looks like a ghost town; no one is standing, and the dead bodies are everywhere.

"Where are all the Nopolyens' kids? What happened to them?!"

"Harley, I'm really proud of you, man. About the kids here, my men established kids' activities all over the city just before my Ants' attack. The real activities were to take the kids out of the city using the same trucks we saw before."

"But the ExA wouldn't let your men use their trucks! And what about the security guards?"

"We always have our ways; and I guarantee you that they'll be safe."

After a few minutes of walking, Finley stops and hides behind the corner, telling us to hide like him.

"What is it?" I whisper.

"We have new friends here!" Finley points to fully armored soldiers who have pale green uniforms on.

"According to the VI, these are Nopoly national guards," Jollya utters.

"We have to wait until the way is clear," Finley says quietly and continues, "Jollya, read the folders that Lisa gave to your husband, quickly, please; we may get some information from them." And Jollya nods yes.

Ten minutes later, the guards have gone; and Finley informs Jollya that we have to move on. At that statement, Jollya closes the folders angrily.

"What's wrong, sis?" the boss asks Jollya, but she doesn't give any response. She sits still on the metal ground.

"Honey, are you okay? What did you read?" I ask her impatiently.

Jollya starts crying while she takes my hands, and then she says, "Do you think that Lori has been treated as a child in this inhumane environment?"

My brain has stopped working, and my hands are shaking. "What do you mean . . . by that, Jollya?"

She looks at me with so many mixed feelings in her eyes: sadness, fear, and anger. She says in a breaking voice: "Do you remember Birth Away technology?"

"Yes . . ."

"It was nothing but a fake! The huge number of kidnapped kids in the lab was the tool for this lie. Nopolyen parents, who gave their babies in the fetal stage to the doctor, have received the kidnapped children who have been taken from their real parents. And . . . and to make sure that all the children would fit into this new environment, the VI system was applied on these kids..."

I find myself dumbfounded by the idea of involving innocent children in all this madness. "Why? Just why?" I scream.

"And what did happen to the babies that have been taken from the Nopolyens?" Finley asks in a broken voice.

Jollya gives no answer, and it feels that my beautiful lady's spirit has disappeared.

"These poor babies have been used in the genetic experiments to come up with the Super Army; an army of superhumans who don't die or get affected by any chemical/ radioactive materials." Jollya stops, seeming to remember something else; and she continues, "I read something about the Perfect Mind. There is a program requesting a clear, pure, young, and creative mind. This reminds me of what BioID requested from Sharon Hospital!"

Finley gets on his knees, shocked and distressed, but his feelings are nothing comparing with mine, which are mixed with so much anger and dread when I heard something related to Lori.

I'm walking towards the First Building, blinding myself from anything but my intention: saving my daughter. And the statue of a man holding a sword in his right hand and an unequal balance in the other becomes clear in the distance; it looks like the other seven statues that contained the Plonsters!

"Stop! Don't move!" A voice brings me back to the world around me to see a bunch of National Guards aiming at me.

"Don't shoot, we are doctors here," I say, trying to lie to avoid dying quickly.

They're moving slowly toward us, and their guns are on me. One of them lowers his weapon and says, "Doctors or outsiders, you are dead either way for not staying home." And they all prepare to shoot. The first shot draws many shots. I'm not falling, but they do with their guns, and the police were the shooters; they come running to me.

"Thank you, sir. I told them that we are doctors."

“You are a doctor in lying—and don’t call me sir, because we are brothers.”

Now I got it; they are the Free Rebels.

“Thank you, and good luck!” I say to them before they go, after leaving extra guns with us.

“You have to be wiser and sharper because next time, we may not face the nice ones,” Finley says seriously.

A couple of minutes after Finley’s lesson, we have reached the area, but there are huge numbers of soldiers around the statue and the building.

“What do we have to do now?” I ask while I’m taking off the binoculars.

“I didn’t expect these numbers of soldiers. I don’t know!” Finley answers with a trembling voice.

“Can’t we use the hologram thing?” Jollya proposes.

“Look at them! They are using infrared, so the emulator hologram is not going to work with them.”

“So how are we going to get in, in that case? It would be a good idea if you borrowed some of the Rebels,” I utter irritated.

“My men are meant to free the children in normal places. Not to save a child in a freaking palace!” Finley says angrily.

I scream out loud, cursing everything and everyone.

“Are you trying to let them catch us again? Jollya, shut his mouth before it kills us!” Finley says angrily before an earthquake with high pressure shakes the whole city, and four huge explosions follow it, making the ground tremble.

“What’s going on?” I ask Finley while closing my eyes and putting my hands on my head, unconsciously trying to stop the tinnitus I got and the sound of crashing glass in my ears.

“I don’t know.”

“Look up there!” Jollya shouts pointing to huge explosions on the top of the city’s wall.

“I believe that came from the Plonsters,” I suggest, looking at the fire mixed with so much smoke.

“Why did they explode?” Jollya asks.

“I don’t know what is going on in this crazy city. All I know that we have to hurry to the building to see Lori in the last possible place she might be hidden,” Finley replies.

While we are running, the voice in the city starts giving orders again, saying:

“Kill everyone out, Eeekesh Wassch . . . protect yourselves from the terrorist outsiders, Aeewsesh Esch . . . end the terrorism.” And the mad orders end finally.

“Guys, we are the terrorists now!” Finley says with a sarcastic laugh.

The National Guards have detected us and start shooting at us while we try to hide from the deadly bullets. We start shooting back to hold them back, but I stop shooting when I get shot in my shoulder, and my hand drops the gun. “Ah! Damn it!” I scream from the pain I’m feeling right now.

“Harley! Nooo! Baby, baby, you’ll be all right, don’t worry!” Jollya says, crying, as she tries to stop the bleeding from my left shoulder.

"Don't take out the bullet now! Just stop the bleeding, and I'll try to stop them from approaching us as much I can," Finley says while shooting.

The pain is indescribable; I feel like my heart will stop beating from the intensity of the pain. But something has definitely stopped: Finley's shooting.

"The sky is falling!" he shouts, right before a huge piece of glass shatters onto the ground, deafening us and increasing the pain in my head. Many pieces of different sizes have followed the first falling one; they reveal the real dark-red sky with its lightning and crushing on the broken ground.

"What now?" I shout, trying to hide with Jollya from the falling glass sky.

"We have to go into the building!" Finley exclaims.

"What about the soldiers?" Jollya asks.

"Many of them have been smashed. We'll face the same fate if we'll just stay here!" Finley replies.

Nothing is going as planned. I know this for a fact when a massive mech lands in front of us, heaving the broken sky of Nopoly up with the bricks and stones; the impact threw us a few meters as well before we land roughly on the ground. This giant heap of scrap looks like the Planster that Jollya had used to help me escape from Nopoly.

"Plonster! Where are your super-duper Ants? Isn't their job to stop any kind of electricity?" I scream.

"My Super-Nano Ants attack specific areas, including these huge things, but they can't hold against the high rad—" and a smash from a big metal hand stops Finley from talking and almost stops my heart.

“This thing seems unhappy about our being here,” I comment. I’m barely walking, with a hole in my head and a bullet in my arm. I can handle all this suffering, but the idea of being kept away from Lori by a big iron killing machine is much more painful. Why do the strong make decisions at the expense of the most basic, simple rights of the weak—to be with their child, for example?

A push from Jollya stops the discussions I had with myself. “It is aiming at us. Run!” Jollya screams hysterically.

Everything in that metal owl is huge—its wings, body, and gun. The rockets that come from the gun are destroying everything and throwing us from left to right with the debris. It starts shooting us in every direction until I am knocked down by the last rocket, which exploded nearby.

“I can’t move anymore,” I mumble. “I’m so dizzy and tired . . . and . . .”

“Honey! I can carry you on my back. We have to move, now!” my guardian angel says. She starts calling Finley to help her carry me, but it seems that Finley is not here!

“Jollya, baby! I love you . . . forever; I’ll never forget that feeling or your angel face. Please, don’t get yourself killed. That damn Finley and I are pretty much dead now. Go and find Lori; tell her that I—”

“No!” Jollya interrupts me, crying and holding me tightly. “We will save her together; I told you before that I’ll never leave you,” this crazy, sweet Jollya continues while the Plonster works on removing the roof we are hiding under.

Thousands of ideas are coming to my head, but the most important one is, who will save Lori if the three of us have died? Will Sami or that Lisa do that? I don’t think so.

The mech starts moving irregularly, and it seems that it's being subjected to electric shocks.

"Guys go into the building. Hurry! Aaaah!" A shaky voice comes from the massive machine after it smashes the building's entrance, opening it. It's Finley!

"Finley! What are you doing in that machine?" I shout with all my might.

"Goooo and find her!" is all he says. There is so much pain in his voice.

"I'll never forgive you if you die because of that stupid thing!" I utter while walking with Jollya's help.

Just before we enter the building, I turn to tell Finley to come out of that scrap and join us, but the Plonster just flies away so fast that I can't catch up to thank him.

"Where is he going?" I exclaim.

A massive explosion, which turns the machine into black smoke and fire with small pieces of fallout, was the answer.

"Noooo! Finley!" Jollya screams.

"Why did he do that . . . why?" I ask, astonished about what happened. Jollya drags me inside the building, and I receive no answer from my crying wife.

20. Inside the First Building

After getting inside the First Building, we enter the washroom to clean ourselves up. This place is totally protected against disasters, even nuclear ones, so we take our gas masks off. I fall on my knees, still shocked and nearly broken.

"Harley, get up! Don't let our friends' sacrifices be in vain!" Jollya's tears motivate me to never give up, so I get up.

While we search the rooms, Jollya recognizes a sound coming from a huge room with many glass containers, which contain different types of bodies. A broken Dictaphone has started playing by itself, speaking with a lot of static and breaking up: ". . . a science award for discovering that human flesh is totally ok to be e—"

"Please, stop it!" I shout quickly, and she turns it off. "I hate the idea that I ate . . . you know. But . . . did you?" I ask Jollya, breathing heavily, and she shakes her head no.

"Only people who were under Bezman's illusion ate the . . . that flesh."

"Why didn't you tell me the first time you saw me in the damn city?" But Jollya doesn't respond; she just looks at me as if she is telling me: you answer it!

She did the right thing by drawing me slowly out of the city. If she had made me face reality then, when my mind was confused and controlled, I'd have taken her to prison in the best-case scenario.

"I avoided telling anyone about this inhumane fact just for your sake. I knew that you'll blame yourself for something you had no clew about, but Finley was smart enough to suspect that something was wrong with the meals when I insisted not to eat and not to let them test the food."

"I'm . . . I'm sorry, babe. I'm an idiot sometimes, but no matter what, I still love you."

Jollya touches my hand, smiling to let me know it's OK, and then she says, "Do you want to hear the 'About Nopoly' note?" And I nod yes, knowing that she wants to change the subject. Jollya changes the recording on the Dictaphone and starts gathering the tools she needs to heal my wounds. The machine starts speaking: "Manuel Stallen, sixth of May, 2078. Thanks to the Liberated Builders, the live-in project has been officially . . . a decade of working on it. Nopoly will be able to be inhabited by only the superior race, as it says in the—"

"Superior race, wow!" Jollya interjects before the voice resumes:

"Manuel Stallen, Nopoly, the tenth of June 2079. The V-Server is fitting perf . . . Bezman system. The only problem . . . be old so sooner than . . . and that's why we are working to find the immortal state on hu . . ."

"We have to destroy the server he talked about after saving Lori; I believe that another Nopoly will exist, with all its madness, if we leave that server active." Jollya agrees while she prepares the bag of fluids and the blood transfusion bag.

"V-Server! Immortal state!" Jollya keeps repeating while the recording is playing talking about the Virtual Illusion with so much static.

"My beautiful nurse will not anesthetize me, right? I'll take the pain in order not to lose my strength," I mumble.

"No, no! Just local anesthetic, honey." And she chooses another audio note, saying:

"Creator We!" She waves the note before she puts the gloves on.

"Manuel Stallen, Nopoly, twentieth of October 2079. This environment is what we dreamed of . . . a loyal nation with one way of thinking, one culture, one color, and one purpose: to live the life we have created. No more . . ." and the man's words are garbled.

"It's out!" Jollya says, showing me the bloody bullet.

"Eh, thank you, babe." Jollya looks at me and gives me her beautiful smile, and I continue, "Let me satisfy my curiosity and start another record, please."

"OK, OK! Stay still! Let's hear Nopoly's Awards for Peace and Science!"

"No, no, no, no! Please, don't!"

"The one that causes laughter is the most tragic disaster," Jollya is laughing through her tears. "I mean, who would think that someone did horrible things or came out with an awful idea would get an award, and not just any award but the Award for Peace and Science, haha," she continues in that creepy manner.

The voice says, "Manuel Stallen with Dr. Vice Osten, ninth of November 2079. We have found a way to increase violence in humans by adding the chromosome from the gorilla Saba, which was genetically modified. The problem is that editing affects the platelets and . . . we'll do it anyway."

"Why did you stop it?" I ask Jollya, who is preparing to stitch up my wound.

"They're the real demons. I don't want to hear this sickness anymore. All I want to hear is something about Lori," Jollya replies. She chooses an note in a hurry and starts to stitch my arm. I feel pain that I don't want to show to my wife; she better finish this quickly to move on.

It takes a long time before a voice starts speaking: "Mathew Navy with Edward Behenna, Nopoly, nineteenth of March 2081. We have developed the system of . . . not be hacked or used by the outsiders anymore because they will be stuck inside it, and it'll explode directly with them . . . is not registered as a Plonster Rider. The amazing thing is the exploded Plonster can—" The playback is stopped by Jollya, who seems angry and shocked.

"That explains why Finley flew away before. . ." Jollya's sad voice trails off.

"For what did he sacrifice himself? Are we that important to him?" I exclaim in astonishment.

"No, not for us." She looks at me with red eyes. "We are ready to go; let's go to find Lori." And she starts running forward before a voice stops us both in our tracks.

"Who the hell are you?"

It's a soldier with two doctors, who are coming towards me holding Jollya's arms. I have to do something, anything, but what can a lying man with a half-broken arm and broken mind do? I have only my weakness to let go.

"I and my man are inhabitants here, and we came here to cure him; we're soldiers." Jollya tries to seem honest with all the shiver in her voice.

"What's your code?" the soldier shouts.

I turn to the left, ignoring all the pain and trying to get up to say: "It's: B.Y." And in a second, I grab my gun from the holster and shoot that soldier a couple of shots, allowing Jollya to handle it after I fall on the bench again, "E."

"On your knees!" Jollya's shouting makes me feel safe. "Honey, are you OK?" she adds.

"I'm fine," I say, trying to get up again with the help of my love.

The doctors look scared and sweaty; their hands are shaking as they kneel beside their soldier's dead body. "Please, don't kill us; we will do whatever you want, please," one of them says, crying.

"One question: Where is Lori Woodman?" I ask them aggressively. "She's our daughter, so please tell us."

"Lori is... in the Future Kid La—" a shot stops his lie.

"Here! She is here, I swear!" The other doctor says dreadfully.

"I know that she is here, but here *where*?" I retort.

"Up in the highest room of this building."

"Lisa didn't lie, then. Come show me the way," I say, aiming at his head.

"I wish I could, but they will realize that the First Building is broken into, and they will take Lori to Querrace."

"Que . . . what?"

"It's a colony in the up high . . ."

"Space?" I ask that doctor, who answers yes.

"I have to contact Dinis and tell him that everything is still fine before he takes your daughter away. You can wait for me to help you get through as soon as I finish the call."

"I'll wait no more," I decide.

"OK then, you go, and I'll call Dinis calmly."

"Give me a reason to trust you, doc!" I prepare the gun with my finger on the trigger.

"Wait! I'll give you two reasons. I'm Paul Wave." He tries to shake my hand, but when I refuse the handshake, he turns to the right, picks up two injections from the side table, then turns back to the man that is aiming at him, ready to shoot.

"First, take this gun away from my head, please, and take these two injections; the purple one will make you stronger, but be wary, because your heartbeat will increase unbelievably, and some biological changes will happen to you in general. The yellow one will get you back to your normal state. No time for more explanation, so just use them when you need to. I hope this atone for my mistakes."

I take the two injections from this doctor, saying:

"And the second reason?"

"There is a door at the end of that hall; the door will lead you to a maze. All you need to pass that maze is to give the right answers."

"Did we have to trust him?" I ask Jollya after leaving the doctor behind.

"Sometimes there is no other choice but counting on someone's humanity."

"Right," I agree.

“I have a question for you, honey; why did you talk to yourself when you were under the VI effect?”

“I . . . I was convincing myself about the new lifestyle that I lived, and I tried making my brain believe what was obvious in the city.”

“I bet the talker did help, too,” Jollya smiles while winking at me.

This Jollya . . . I love her; I truly do. She always has my back and never gives up on me in my stupidity.

“Jollya! Have I told you how much I love you?”

“Haha, no . . . I guess.”

I tell her, “Your love is my universe.”

“And only God knows how much I love you.”

“Wait, do you really believe in God?” I exclaim.

“Yes, and I was studying religions the last couple years before the nuke war,” she says.

“What makes you waste your time with false myths?”

“Finley. His attitude makes me curious about his religion. Will that change your feelings toward me?”

“I mean as long as you’re not radical, it’s . . . fine for me,” I respond.

“To be radical is an idea, not a religion. Remember that we, white American parents, were terrorists in the eyes of the Nopoly government, just because we didn’t follow the rules that kept their inhumane acts secret,” Jollya says.

“I do agree that they are the real radical—”

"They know they are, and they want to hide their shame by throwing it on the oppressed ones, who can't take anymore and have to react," Jollya interrupts me emotionally.

"Innocent guilty principle," I respond.

We stop walking when we come to a door that has an "MM" sign.

"This should be the door that Paul talked about," she says.

"Let's get in," I say excitedly as I open the metal door. The room we enter is so dark and closed in all directions, but the roof is open, showing us the endless darkness.

"It made of very heavy metal!" I comment, knocking on the walls.

"All we need to pass it is to be ho—"

"Welcome to the Moral Maze." A shining eye has illuminated the room with yellow light. "The right answer will open the right door; the wrong one will mislead you inside of me. No way to get out and no way to break my walls. Let's get started!" That eye says with a really creepy voice, "Question one: What is the purpose of building Nopoly?"

I look at Jollya, who seems dumbfounded by this thing, and then I answer: "To contain the superior race!"

The room becomes illuminated with red by the eye at the same time it says, "Wrong! Enter the room on your right." And the eye turns off its light while the wall on the right raises, revealing an illuminated room.

"What? Isn't right that they . . . eh, damn it!"

"Let's move on honey," Jollya says while she walks into the next room.

"Question two: What is the tool that we use to blind people to the truth?"

"Fear."

"What?" I shout at Jollya, who seems unsure.

A green light comes from the eye as it says, "Correct. Enter the room behind you." And the wall behind has opened.

"Isn't better to go further?" I interrupt Jollya's little celebration.

"Forward and backward, this is the life." Jollya shrugs her shoulders as if to ask me what else we can do.

The eye continues. "Question three: What is the process to control the human brain?"

"The VI mask—" I answer hastily.

"Wrong! go the room on your left."

The front wall rotates while the left wall opens.

"Why? What is the right answer then?" Jollya made no answer and gets in the next room that has a rotating back wall, which is parallel to the front rotating wall in the room we were in. And the open wall is closing now.

"Question one: What is the purpose of building Nopoly?"

"Are you kidding me?" I exclaim.

"Wrong! Enter the room in front of you."

"Aaaah! I wish I could kill you!"

"Harley! No time to waste fighting with this thing. At least we are not going backward," Jollya says, winking at me. I feel so dumb. I couldn't calm down until I smashed the iron wall.

“Question four: Why are children so important to us?” asks the eye.

“They are the future and can be formed easily, whatever way you want,” Jollya answers without hesitation.

“Correct. Enter the room on your left,” it says, and we leave the triangular room for a bit bigger room.

“Question five: What do females mean to us?”

“The other half of the community?” I jump with this obvious answer.

“Wrong! Enter the room behind you.” I kneel, full of anger and hate toward this stupid maze.

“They are clearly wasting our time to take her away!” I shout and hit the ground as hard as I can.

“Harley, we can pass this maze; just calm down and don’t lose your patience.” Jollya takes my hand to get me up and move to the next room.

“Question six: What is running us?”

I’m thinking about money, but Jollya grabs my hand, whispering, “I got this.” And then she turns to the eye and says, “Satan.”

I exclaim, “Seriously? Now, you become superstitions be—”

“Correct. Enter the room on your left.”

Jollya is looking at me as if to tell me I’m dumb, heh.

“Look I was mind-controlled by the VI, just like you are now by superstition myths!”

“No, I’m not. Finley taught me a lot of things that are hidden from you, which you have to accept!”

“I don’t want to know them, thanks,” I retort.

“Well, at least it was the right answer and that explains even more things to me.”

We enter the next room. I feel so anxious to know when we will be done with these stupid damn questions.

“Question seven: What is the limit for us?”

After a few seconds, Jollya answers confidently, “There is no limit.” And a correct answer takes us to the front room. That feels good to go just further.

“Question eight: Who can’t we control and must be terminated?”

“Eeeh—”

“Smart people who can think and criticize,” I interrupt Jollya as she is about to answer.

“Wrong! Enter the room on your right.”

“No, no, no. This is bullshit!” I say, looking at the upset Jollya. “I got it. I’m sorry. You are the boss now; I give up with this . . .” I trail off.

“Question five: What do females mean to us?”

“A desire,” Jollya answers angrily with tears in her eyes.

“Correct. Enter the room in front of you.”

I hug Jollya and ask, “Jollya, are you okay, honey?”

“I’m fine,” my beautiful wife replies with a small smile.

"Question nine: For what reason are you here?" Jollya directs her eyes to me and nods, telling me to answer this.

"We are here for Lori Woodman." I respond this time with full confidence.

"Correct. Enter the elevator."

Jollya and I share the same expression: the look of hope and confidence that we'll gain seeing our daughter and saving her.

As soon as we rise in the glass elevator, the huge dark maze appears down below.

"I bet that I would've spend days . . . maybe months in these rooms without you!" I look at Jollya gratefully for being with me when I need her—in fact, I need her all the time.

"I hope that Lori is good. Hold on, baby; we are coming!" I add, brushing aside my romantic feelings.

21. A Little Hope

The elevator is open now, and my heart feels open as well for the first time; all I want is to see my daughter safe and rescue her from this place. I promise that I will always be beside her, sit with her while she paints, and then put her on my shoulders when she wants to fly.

"Don't worry, my little angel, we are coming," I express with all the emotions for all the moments I wasted with the material world, instead of spending my time with Lori.

After a long walk in the hall, we face a statue of a person wearing a very old plague mask on his face. We hide behind the statue, which holds in one hand a mask that reminds me of my VI mask and points forward with the other hand.

"Look over there! There is an agent in every room," I whisper.

"And one is walking, there," Jollya adds.

As we are hidden behind the statue, we move around it a little bit to stay out of sight of the moving agent. Luckily, the others are standing still, looking disturbed.

Jollya takes out something from her bag, saying:

"This is a little gift from Finley."

"A capsule? Is it a euthanizing one?"

"A double-side capsule; inside one of the sides are hundreds of tiny insects called the Small Consumers," she says.

"How is that supposed to help us?" I ask.

Jollya opens one side of the capsule and drips a couple of drops on her hand, and then, she wipes her hands all over her face and body. "Do like I did, hurry!" she says, and then she drips some of that stinky liquid on my hands.

"When are we going to be consumed?"

"They will be," Jollya says, opening the other side of the capsule and throwing it into the air. A couple of minutes later, screams come from everywhere in the place.

"Itchy, it's so itchy! Damn it!" And then the voices turn to gargles. I have a fleeting thought about what if Finley used these insects as a punishment against the society, but instead of that, he used the Nano Ants to avoid harming innocents, maybe . . .

"That Finley was really a madman!" I exclaim in a shrill voice.

"His madness was nothing compared to this government. All he did was react, like what we're doing now."

She is right, absolutely right! I would never think to break the law if my daughter was safe; in fact, I would attack anyone who didn't obey the law. I wouldn't feel what the law-breaker is feeling, and I would never understand his or her viewpoint.

"Let's separate to look for Lori. If one of us finds Lori, we get the hell out of here," I say.

"And how are we going to go out of this secure building?"

"I have a little bomb that will make a huge explosion, opening a path to escape by a rope," I say, thanking Finley in my heart. I take out a gun with a silencer and tell Jollya, "Use it when you need to. Now go to the rooms on the right, and I'll go to the ones on the left." And we get moving.

I give peace to the tortured ones by giving them mercy bullets. While I'm taking the security card from one of the dead agents, a room draws my attention. Many wires and screens cover the room, which has a bench with a machine full of wires above it in the middle of the cold room.

Many notes are on the table, but one of them has a picture of my daughter! It's talking about . . . the V-Server. What is the relevance between the server and our daughter?

I read, "'Every creation needs a brain, and the V-Server is the brain of Nopoly. A little brain can build a whole world. The experience has succeeded, and the Bezman System proves its effectiveness.' What does that even mean?"

I exit the room impatiently searching in every room for Lori, who is not in any of them.

"Jollya! Have you found her?" I call out.

"No, but I found this." Jollya gives me a folder, and her face is wet with tears.

"Brain surgery! What? Where is she, *where*?" I shout, turning in all directions.

"This door, we . . . we didn't go in it." I point at a sliding door.

After we get inside, the doors on both sides close, and we get sprayed by a gas. A couple of seconds later, the door opens on the other side.

"Here, we have to search here," I begin, and then a girl's scream comes from the right side of the hall.

"There!" Jollya shouts, and we start running toward the shouts that keep coming.

All the way, my legs never stop running, and my heart beats even faster; in addition, my gun never stops shooting any agent who shows his face to me.

"Lori! Where are you, baby?" And a scream comes as a response to me; so I run toward the door that her voice comes from. I smash through it and shove the nurse, who was trying to block the door.

"Jollya, lock the door now!" I say after getting inside the surgery room and ending the nurse's life.

A bound, gagged young woman who looks scared as hell, surrounded by three doctors, is in the middle of the room; one of the doctors has an injection ready to give to the girl."

"Wha . . . where is my daughter, Lori Woodman?" I exclaim.

The doctor I addressed looks at me, removing the magnifier from in front of his eyes and responding with a trembling voice, "This is a sterile area for surgery. You shouldn't be here, sir!" But a bullet ends his worries about our presence.

"Don't worry, girl; I won't kill you." I try to be nice to the young lady, who is shaking all over from fear. Jollya takes it a step further by releasing the scared lying girl, ignoring the shocked, terrified doctors.

"Where is Lori Woodman?" I ask the second doctor slowly.

"She is . . . not here. I belie—" And a shot ends the same damn lie I heard earlier.

"Where is she?" I shout, ignoring Jollya's calls.

The old doctor raises his shaking hands, telling me not to shoot. “I know where your daughter is, but let me explain everything before you—”

“Speak!” I interrupt him aggressively.

The doctor lowers his hands and says, “Your daughter has a very beautiful mind, a creative one, which can build a whole beautiful world. A nineteenth-century style world, which Dinis needed for a closed city that doesn’t need cars or a very advanced and polluting lifestyle, was the perfect one, and that’s what gives Nopoly its special touch—”

“Why would I care about this? Tell me, where is my daughter? What have you done to her?”

“Harley!”

I look at Jollya and snap, “Not now, Jollya!” And I ignore the rolling tears on the girl’s cheeks.

“Dinis told us to use Lori’s mind to build Nopoly in the Nopolyens’ eyes; that was with the help of his company, BioID, which came up with the Bezman system; all of this happened under the project ‘Live In.’ But the Bezman machine, which was used on Lori, accelerates cell aging by about double . . .”

“So?” I express my confusion with a broken voice, which make this doctor more confident.

“So your daughter is not a little innocent girl anymore,” that filthy old man says in a dirty way.

“Harley! This . . . this is . . . our daughter.” Jollya holds that girl’s hand, kissing her head while she is crying. The second I look at the girl, the damn doctor does something, and the alarm starts in the building, along with red lights.

“Die, you scum!” I finish him directly.

The little girl, or Lori, as that dead doctor said, runs to the corner at the end of the room, terrified.

"Baby, baby, it's me, your mommy, and this is your dad. Do you remember us?"

I move closer to the girl but not close as Jollya. "Am I going crazy or this is for real?" I exclaim. "This girl is at least sixteen! Lori was like . . . six years old the last time she . . . Eh . . ." I stop, considering what that doctor said about the Bezman machine. Jollya begins to sing.

"*I'm looking straight into your eyes,*

Telling you how much you are nice

Such a little cute doll,

With a beautiful pure soul

***

Hush, little Lori, I'm here don't worry

Deep in my heart, I put you with your daddy . . ."

Jollya stops singing when she receives a huge hug from the girl. "Harley, it's her!" she confirms.

The girl looks at me with her eyes red from crying, waiting for me to come back from my thoughts.

"Lori? Is it you?" I say while touching her hands. "The same tune I used to hear in the Temple! Everything makes sense now . . ."

I open the necklace that has Lori's picture in it; the necklace that Jollya gave me in Dallecus before starting our mission to save the kids.

"There is no doubt . . . look at her eyes; they have never changed!"

The girl hugs me, interrupting all my thoughts; and I hug her back. I feel as the warmth in my heart consumes my feelings, except the feeling of longing.

"I can feel it, I swear, I do. You are Lori Woodman; you are my daughter!" And the girl agrees with quiet vocalizations and a little smile on her pale face.

A long hug envelopes my family as a celebration of a family reunion before we hear steps getting closer and closer. Lori starts moving nervously and looking in all directions.

"What are you trying to tell us, Lori?" I ask her, and she tries again with more details and more signs.

"They will take your brain out?" Jollya translates the signs, and Lori is nodding yes.

"Don't worry, sweetheart, as long as we're breathing, we won't leave you again," I say confidently.

I start knocking on the walls to know which one is most vulnerable, and I think I detect it, so I look at Jollya saying:

"Honey, let her wear the suit that's hanging there. Put the gas mask on her face, and put your gas mask on as well."

With difficulty, I put a mask on and take out the little bomb from my pocket.

"Back off and hide!" I shout before sticking that bomb on the wall. A huge vibration shocks the atmosphere and moves the table we hide behind. That explosion opens up about a fifty-inch hole, which shows us the ruined Nopoly.

The door is getting pounded so hard; at the same time, I'm binding the rope to use it to get down. Just before I look down to see if the thirty-meter rope has reached the ground below, the door gives way. Two soldiers aim guns at us, and a man with an old plague mask and black elegant suit is between the soldiers; my gun is pointed at the middle one, who looks to be the boss, with zero doubt to shoot him. This masked gentleman reminds me of that statue we saw before.

"Well, that wasn't expected. Guys, get the guns down! It's not how we treat our guests," that creepy gentleman says, pushing his soldiers' guns down. "I want to apologize for their behavior, but we thought that some crazy people got into the surgery room."

"Who are you?" I ask, keeping my gun on them.

"My name is David, and you?"

"It's not your business; I'm here to take my daughter and leave."

"Your daughter?" he exclaims.

"Yes, my daughter, Lori."

"This girl is nothing but a clone from your daughter."

"What?" I shout.

"I mean, how is it possible that your six-year-old daughter could become seventeen in like a year and three months?"

I look at the shocked Jollya and the scared girl, considering his speech.

"Honestly, this is the server for Nopoly, but she is not Lori. In fact, your daughter is living in a suite, taking her medicines and becoming better every day, thanks to Dinis—"

"Dinis!" I shout, full of rage.

Lori asks, "How can we trust you? I feel that it's my daughter, and you are—"

"Excuse me, madam, but your feelings are incorrect."

"A mother's feeling is stronger than your lies," Jollya says angrily.

"She is emotional," the masked doctor says. "Leave them and come to see your real daughter."

My weakness is my curiosity, and I can't push it aside. There is a 1 percent possibility that he is telling the truth, and I really want to know where my real daughter is. In addition, I really want to see that Dinis and gouge out his throat.

I turn to Jollya. "Honey, I'll come back. I just—"

"Harley, please don't . . ."

"Baby, I just want to make sure that everything is . . . right. I'll come back, I promise!" and I give the girl a pat on her hair. I turn to the others. "Move yourselves, and I'll follow. Any stupid move, and your boss is dead . . ."

We exit the surgery room and start walking in the hall. "Why do you have that ugly old mask?" I ask.

"The secret for that mask is in this question: Was the bacterium *Yersinia pestis* made by God? God is considered good, right? So why would God create something terrible for humankind?"

"I don't know . . . and I don't care," I respond.

"The black death was the bath to achieve glory in this country by exterminating all the savages from this land. Actually, material gain was the motivation in the first place."

"Shout your damn mouth!" I exclaim.

"OK, just let me tell you a secret: unlike you, I do believe in a God, but it's a material one: it's money!"

"Is that your purpose in life? Who are you really?"

"I am the one who will give you back your daughter . . . I'm Dinis."

"I knew it, you liar. Keep moving!"

I swear that I'll make him beg to die peacefully; I just want to see if there is any chance to reveal the truth. But there is a question I have had in my head for a while, and it's consuming my thinking; I can hold it no more.

"What is your relevance to the American government?" I ask.

He turns to me while we're walking, saying:

"You know, we are not the type of people who control the governments like what the conspiracy theories always say. We make the rules for these governments, including yours. So please, do not have any hard feelings against the policy of your lovely America."

I stop moving when we get close to the cleaning room. "I'm not going in with you. Bring me the girl, and your head will still be able to keep planning great, glorious plans!" I tell him.

No one moves, so I get angrier and shoot the wall beside one of the soldiers.

"No need to use violence! Bunim, go and bring us the Tearer," Dinis orders one of his soldiers.

"What is Tearer? Don't play with me; I swear I'll blow your mind with one bullet!" I exclaim.

He raises his hands, clarifying, "We call her that because she is always crying because of missing being a normal kid—"

“Stop!” I interrupt him to stop myself from getting emotional here and now.

“Her tears were always rolling and rolling, and that’s why we call her the—”

“I said stop!” And I shoot beside Dinis’s head.

“That wasn’t a miss, I know it. You don’t want to kill me because with one more kill, your humanity is drowned in blood.”

“You say that as if your hands are clean!”

“That’s why I have gloves on, to keep my hands clean. Some of the politicians are like fancy gloves to us; we move them with our hands, and they are the ones who get stained by the blood of the savages,” this scum says, laughing.

He’s trying to provoke me, and he has succeeded, but I have to keep calm until I find my real daughter. Whether he is lying or not, he’s a dead man for what he did—for all the kids who have been taken from their families, for all the innocent people who have been killed for no reason but being different, and for the damn Finley, who sacrificed himself while he was helping to find Lori.

The ground starts shaking as an earthquake has started in the place.

“What is that?” I ask, ready to press the trigger.

“Don’t freak out; the weather outside is not always stable,” that creep says.

Suddenly, the whole building is shaking, and a loud cracking sound comes from the ceiling. In a second, the ceiling gets removed by a huge metal machine; it’s the Plonster showing up with its iron owl face.

"You liar!" I start shooting at Dinis. But that scum is standing still behind a metal hand that is stretched from that Plonster, which is protecting him. He shouts, "This is your little hope, hahaha!"

I throw the empty gun, terrified about what could happen next in this situation. The red reflection from this Plonster's eyes above the rain of falling rocks makes me freak the hell out and run like crazy while Dinis gives orders to take Lori to Querrace.

Jollya was right. I should've listened to her and not trusted that well-dressed man. What should I do now? Most important is to get Jollya and Lori out of this place, but the problem is the Plonster, which is chasing me with its red eyes.

I enter the room, shouting to Jollya to get out of there, but there is no Jollya here or Lori. I notice the rope is moving a little bit, so I assume they are escaping. I make sure that they are doing it by watching Jollya sliding down with Lori on her back.

"They are coming. Run away and use the flare to call the rebels!" I scream with all my power.

"This is the time to be a hero of my story for once. I'm already dead, so let's make it worth it; let's give my family a chance to live in peace." I'm talking to myself while emptying the purple injection into my veins.

More rocks are falling while that Plonster keeps removing the ceiling and searching for my daughter.

"Little hope, just a little hope, please!" I keep repeating while I'm surrounding with rubble and drowning in the darkness under them. Why didn't the injection do anything different in me? Was he lying? How many times do I have to be deceived? First my normal life before the crisis, second my life in Nopoly, then that damn Dinis, and finally the last hope I have with this injection. Why? Whom can I trust when Jollya isn't with me, or rather if no one is with me?

I wasn't expecting to live the experience of the people who were under the rubble. People who lived in wars in the past and got stuck under their own home's rocks—that was strange to imagine, and I never felt any pity for them, yet here I am, living their terrible experience and feeling a part of what they felt.

A sound wakes my brain, saying:

"Here, put her here! And take the little one up as I told you."

"No!" I try to scream while I'm gathering my strength, which suddenly feels boosted, so I start removing the rubble piece by piece till I find the way out. My muscles feel so much stronger that my jump is three times higher!

"Don't, please!" I hear Jollya and begging before a shot mutes that crying sound, and I stop for a moment, looking up to see the flying Plonster is flying away.

"Lori! No, no, no!"

In a split second, my heart starts beating so fast that it shakes my head, and I feel the worst possible pain in my stomach and so much heat feels underneath my skin; but then, I see the worst sight I can possibly see in my entire life . . .

"Jollyaaa!"

I jump down to the broken ground, like a monster that has lost its princess; and I see my wife's blood covering her. I have no concentration on anything but running to her.

When I reach her, I fall on my knees, trying to wake her and begging her to not leave me alone. But she doesn't answer me. Jollya, my love . . . is gone. It's not her fault or mine. This world is cruel, so cruel and full of violence, so whenever we really love another human, we'll die, leaving the one we love crying in this dirty, filthy world.

I'm giving Jollya, my faithful, loving wife, what is probably the last hug, promising to try to correct my faults till I become a truly loving human being.

I send up a sign for any Free One to come and bury my love, because this fight might be my final one. A kiss I give to my beautiful dead love behind the masks we used to breathe a clean air; I wish they would come out with a mask to clean our souls from evil. Talking about evil—that damn Dinis is running away from the destruction.

With long, fast steps passing all the rubble and the crushed soldiers, I chase Dinis, who enters a room that has a drop-down concrete door. I grab a thick rock and throw it under the concrete door, and it gets stuck under the door, leaving a gap for my crazed self; and as I slide under the door, I find myself in a room that has a couple of little rocket ships.

Dinis quickly opens the little gate of one rocket ship, looking terrified at seeing me, and he gets inside the rocket. The ship is getting started, and the smoke starts rising, and everything is ready. I start pulling the gate with all my force, prying it open.

"Don't, please! Ahhh . . . All you want . . . I can give you everything you want; I can tell you the secret of life . . ." Dinis starts freaking out when I throw him out of the ship after opening the gate.

"My wife is dead, and all I want is to get my life back. You have nothing to do but end lives, but there is still a little hope . . . my flying hope," and I point up at Lori. "Considering that you didn't kill my little hope, I won't shoot you," I say, throwing the gun away. I hear his babbled thanks, but I turn to him again, saying:

"But you've killed my love." And the first punch breaks his mask, revealing his real face; skinny, blue-eyed, and beardless.

"Finley is dead," and I deliver another smash, "Alexa," a punch, "and all the demons we killed who weren't damn demons."

I keep hitting his nasty face till it is crushed. I'm not satisfied yet, but I have work to complete, so I leave this rubbish.

I get inside the ship quickly, and then it starts rising, leaving the broken place with a broken face that broke my heart. Before the rocket takes me away, I cast a look at Jollya, who is lying still, facing the open sky. My tears start rolling, blurring my vision. No one compares with her, because she did everything possible to keep me close to the right way and waken to reality. I was the good man she saw through her beautiful eyes, when I was nothing but a dumb, blind, brainwashed man. My guardian angel will never die; she'll always be with me, boosting my goodness, even though she is getting disappearing from sight . . .

As soon as I get closer to the Plonster, I start controlling the rocket, positioning it to hit the underside of the huge machine. I've doubled the speed of the ship twice to reach Lori before she ends up in the space colony. The problem is there isn't enough fuel to get back from this high to the ground, but I'll work it out after saving Lori.

A shock shakes the whole rocket, and my heart starts beating even faster than before. I hit that Plonster successfully, and the ship gets stuck in the machine's downside, which allows me to open the top gate of the ship and get inside the iron monster, which becomes unstable.

"Lori! Where are you, baby? Dad is here!" I shout while moving through the wires and the mechanical parts that I'm ruining with my strength.

I see a little gate getting pushed from the other side, so I creep closer, and with a little pull, I open the gate to see Lori in tears.

"Oh, sweetheart! Don't worry, I will get you out of here, I promise," I say while hugging her nicely.

Carefully, we creep inside this swinging machine till we approach the gate of the ship. Lori gets in first, and I'm about to go after her, but two hands surround my neck from above, stopping me from moving or even breathing. My strength doesn't help me anymore, and it feels like I become paralyzed.

Lori appears to help me, who let her down many times with or without intent, by pulling my powerless arms to her.

"Die, you bastard!" Those words come from the suffocating man; but a rising and falling movement inside the machine makes the other injection fall from my pocket, which Lori takes and injects into the man's hand. The man starts to let go, screaming loudly, and Lori hastily pulls me to her.

"Close the gate with the red button that has a number one. Quickly!" And she does so after signing yes. Since we heard the alarm in the fallen machine, she starts pressing all the buttons, trying to leave the Plonster as fast as possible.

Lori is a smart girl; there is no doubt about it, especially as she knows how to give the ship a push by the pneumatic cannon of the rocket ship, which goes in all directions. And we start moving away from the machine.

A few seconds later, the metal scrap above us explodes, shaking our fallen ship.

"Lori, I can't move myself, so make my arms hug you, please!"

When Lori does so, I get so emotional that my tears start flowing, but that is not the reason for this goodbye hug. I try to remember the song that my love was always singing to Lori.

"*Eh, little Lori, I'm here, don't worry*

Deep in my heart, I put you with Mommy

Be wherever, we're always with you,

Together, and forever for you

We are here together, and . . ."

I start coughing in pain, but I want to say something before I lose my voice.

"Lori, I have no apology to . . . to cover the foolish acts that I did to many people, including the ones I love. I . . . I hope that the actions I did to . . . toward the other kids and you may redeem some of what I did. But . . . always remember, I, and your mom . . . are with you and loving you . . . forever. I have one wish that I want you to fulfill . . . that wish is to—"

A forceful crash stops me from speaking, shaking my body so hard that it feels my bowels are mixed and my bones are broken.

I feel no pain after all that landing. I become so numb from my injuries that my brain can't feel anymore.

Lori starts moving, which makes my day; thankfully, she can move at least to inform me that she is fine.

"Thanks for the hug; are you still OK?" I ask, coughing in pain.

She hugs me and then encourages me to get up. "Dad!"

Lori is speaking! What a feeling! She's calling the one who doesn't deserve her struggle to talk.

"Lori! You really make my day . . . thank you . . . I'm done for now; I can barely move my jaws."

Lori starts moving her head, telling me that she disagrees. She takes my real human hand, which is covered by the suit, and, tapping at it, tells me to be calm.

"I saved you, as I promised." I smile and then continue, "Lori, please forgive me for everything I've done. I love you, your mom loves us, and they love . . ." I can't talk anymore due to all the injuries in my body, and my racing heart makes it feel like my eyes will explode.

With half-open eyes and blurred vision, I see the gate is getting moved, and a bunch of people start looking at me and my daughter.

"Get them out!" someone is shouting from the crowd.

Lori gets out, crying and holding my hand for the last time, I guess, while I saying with tears on my cheeks, "Take . . . care, my . . ."

Lori Woodman

22. The End

A sound wakes me up with the sunlight that comes from the window.

“Dad, dad, wake up, it is too late. Come on!”

How is that possible? Lori is young again, and she can talk normally!

I look around to see that I was sleeping on the couch, which was in our old house we lived in before all the crazy things that happened. Was it a long nightmare? Everything here seems normal as it was!

“Was it a comfortable nap?” Finley utters, sitting in the corner, drinking coffee!

“H . . . how?!”

“Honey! Breakfast!”

I run to the kitchen, and I see her! Jollya is here, and she’s perfectly fine!

“Good morning, honey. You always wake up too late on the weekend, haha. Finley and the others came to congratulate us on our tenth anniversary,” Jollya says, smiling. Finley, Alexa, and the others come in while Lori plays around me happily!

I don’t know what is going on, but I hurry to Jollya and hug her.

“You’re alive!” and I turn to Lori, pick her up, and kiss her on the cheek.

“We are all alive, Harley,” Tavon says, smiling.

“Was it a nightmare? Or is this all a kind of simulation?” I question myself loudly. Jollya looks at me and pats me on the back.

“It was a harsh reality we lived in,” she says.

“So this is a simulation!”

“In your head,” Jollya agrees happily, and she continues, “I always said that I won’t leave you.”

“I don’t mind living in this life, and you are beside me. Thank you, my only love.” And I hug my wife before I turn to the crowd behind me, saying:

“And thanks to all you guys, especially you, boss Finn.”

****

Sami came to the flare spot with the Free Ones, and Harley has been transported to Dallecus to have health treatment. Sami does that in the hope that Harley could get better for Lori’s sake, but Harley went into a coma after all the injuries he got and the blood he lost.

Thanks to the modified Bezman system, Harley will live his short life with his family in his mind till it dies. That was a demand from Lori: to make one of her saviors live a good life, even in the simulation world.

Jollya Woodman has been buried in Dallecus in a tomb that describes her as an important hero of her family, a rebel, a free person, brave, kind, a believer, a faithful wife, a trusted friend, and, most importantly, an affectionate mother.

Lori Woodman has a new normal life to live after being cured from the autism in Dallecus thanks to the scientists there. She begins learning to speaking properly and learning to play piano, and she intends to contribute plans for Dallecus to be a better place for the next generation, the generation that will be the hope to repair broken humanity and bring life on Earth again. But she will never forget her family. She is always visiting her mother's grave and writing books beside her sleeping father forever.

About the author

Faissal Alchaar is an art lover who was born in Syria in 1994. He studied architecture there for two years, but the civil war forced him to leave his friends, relatives, studies, and drawings and moved to Sweden in 2015.

Alchaar is an incisive critic who dislikes halfhearted and incomplete work, so he decided to work hard to create one of the many stories that had stuck in his mind. With this story, *Broken Humanity*, which took a year to complete, could begin his career as an author to publish more stories.

The author is a gamer and likes good stories in games, movies, and anime. Events in the world helped to free his imagination to portray the future, based on our present circumstances and the past that we have left, in Alchaar's perspective.